LUSTY VOYAGE I

By

Jiro Chatelain

JIRO CHATELAIN

ISBN: 978-1-951790-02-8(Paperback)

ISBN: 978-1-951790-03-5(Ebook)

Library of Congress Control Number: **2020904262**

First Edition

Cover and book design by Nanoo Chatelain

Published by:

VOO LAY VOO LLC

Florida, USA

JIRO CHATELAIN

CONTENT WARNING

LUSTY VOYAGE BOOK 1, 2 & 3 contain sexually oriented material intended for individuals 18 years of age or older and of legal age to read sexually explicit material.

Dedication

I dedicate this book to all the amazing women in the world and to all the women who want to discover themselves. I hope this book gives you the courage you need to embrace your sexuality and take your sex life into your hands. Your body is yours, love it and care for it. Your pleasure and your orgasm are important. Don't let anybody tell you otherwise. You are not wanton or immoral if you want to have an orgasm, masturbate or use sex toys.

Author's Note

This book is for every adult woman in the world; Getting a sex toy or using one doesn't make you a promiscuous woman. Instead, it shows that you are a woman who appreciates her body's need and has the courage to fulfill that need. Sex toys don't and shouldn't replace sex with your partner. Sex toys helps to sustain relationships as it can be used to spice up things in the bedroom. As a woman, using a sex toy will help you to know more about your body. It will also prevent unwanted pregnancy and STDS if follow proper hygiene. If you don't own a sex toy, then you are missing out on a lot of explosive pleasures.

I hope you enjoy this book.

QUOTES

Rebecca Hayes (An ardent sex toy fan)-

I had wine in my belly, a finger in my pussy and a dildo in my mouth; what more could I ask for?

Alice Williams (A sex educator)-

Orgasms have been a part of my life since I was a young girl. It was my answer to all life's problems. I gave myself an orgasm for all my little achievements. I gave myself an orgasm when I had a problem, and I didn't know how to solve it. I gave myself orgasms for so many reasons, it's my body and it deserves to be pampered too. Many women give their man orgasms all the time, but they never remember to give themselves one.

Tips from Alice William's Workshop

Do you own a sex toy? Do you want to put some spark in your relationship or take your lady to the peak of her arousal? If you also want to give yourself a good time, you know, have some solo sex, these tips will help you. These are some of the erogenous spots on a woman's body.

- **Lips**
- **Nape/ Ears**
- **Breasts/ Nipples**
- **Back of her legs/ ankle/ feet**
- **Her inner thighs/ Armpits**
- **Stomach**
- **Palms**
- **Butt**

- **Vagina/ Clit**

TABLE OF CONTENS

Prologue

My family was in a big mess. My mother was lying helplessly in a hospital bed after she attempted to take her life. Nana, my grandmother blamed me for Mom's situation. My sex toy collections have brought me an immense joy and pleasure but now I have to get rid of them for the sake of my family. How did I end up in this situation?

How did a Christian girl become a woman who owned collections of sex toys and used them at every opportunity she got? I had gone from being a shy virgin to a woman who played with anal beads and masturbated every night.

Taking my orgasms and pleasure into my hands was a huge step for me, considering my stifling Christian background. Another milestone was when I attended Alice William's sex class. How did a good Christian girl like me end up in a sex class filled with naked women?

I had never taken off my clothes in front of anyone before, but there I was already pulling off my bra and blouse. Yes, I felt a burning shame, but it only lasted for minutes. Alice William's sex class was another adventurous lusty journey for me.

Oh, I blushed to the root of my hair when we all took turns to look at each other's pussy, admired and complimented it.

Choosing between my family and my toys would be a hard choice to make; could I trust myself to make the right decision?

LUSTY VOYAGE I

CHAPTER I

Good Girls Make Good Matches

"*S*arah is pregnant," Mom said, shaking her head.

"She has brought so much shame to her family. She has to marry the boy who got her pregnant; I don't feel sorry for her. Any girl who fornicates should be ready for the consequences."

My cheeks burned as Mom looked at me. We were having dinner when she started talking about my friend, Sarah, who got pregnant out of wedlock. I was from a religious family that considered so many things as a sin. I wasn't allowed to have male friends, attend social events without a chaperone, or have friends outside our religious circle.

"Rebecca is a decent girl," Nana Debby said. My grandmother taught me how to read the Bible, how to pray and she always told me that men loved decent women. I was expected to remain a virgin until my wedding night. Sometimes, the religious doctrines felt like a noose around my neck, but I loved my family, and I didn't want to disappoint them. I loved being a decent girl, I loved wearing decent clothes and I hoped to marry a good man someday and have children.

"We are proud of you, Becky," Dad said. My lips spread into a smile. I felt sorry for Sarah, but I would never disappoint my parents the way she disappointed hers by having premarital sex and falling pregnant. My body was the temple of the Lord, and it was to be kept holy.

Nana Debby, my maternal grandmother, smiled at me again. After dinner, I did the dishes and went into my room to read a motivational book I bought earlier in the day. I lay on my stomach on my bed as I flipped through the first few chapters. The book was talking about God's love and how His children were princesses and princes. I felt a flutter in my heart as I continued to read the book. I was happy to be one of God's children. I was royalty.

Within an hour, I had finished reading the book. I closed the book, said a quick prayer and turned off the lights. There was so much happiness in my heart, knowing that God wanted the best for me. I didn't feel sleepy, so my mind wandered back to the events of the day.

My grandmother and I volunteered at the community orphanage every weekend. I remembered the smile on the faces of the children when they saw the presents, we brought for them. I loved being a part of my Christian community and showing kindness to others.

My family and I lived in a small town called Rock of Roses. Wildflowers and roses surrounded the little town, which was in the midst of beautiful rocks. There was a small river in the town and a hall where most of the town's activities were held. Most of the families in my neighborhood were Christians and we all attended Roses of Rock Chapel, which was in the center of the town.

I was in the choir; my dad was a Deacon in the church and my mother was a deaconess. Nana Debby was one of the Church's elders who counseled the younger people in the church. I grew up in the church, attended every service with my family and volunteered at the church every weekend since I was seven years old. My parents bought a house in **Rock of Roses** after their marriage, the house had six bedrooms, a spacious living room and kitchen. We also had a garden. Nana Debby moved in with us five years ago, after Grandpa Lewis passed away. My parents were strict, but they loved the Lord. So many things were forbidden in our household; swear words and even the mention of sex was a taboo.

My parents never talked to me about the birds and the bees like my classmates' parents did. Some of my friends had started dating but I was waiting for the right time-for the man that God had made for me. Sometimes, I thought about the future, the home I would build with the man God chose for me and the godly children we would have.

Nana's sweet melodic voice filled the air. She was signing a classic Christian song in her room. Nana Debby loved to sing, she had a lovely voice. Mom loved to sing too but she rarely sang now. I started to hum the song as my eyes closed, sleepily.

Chapter II

An Amazing Discovery

The morning was chilly when I woke up. I had a quick shower, ran a comb through my hair and braided it into a single braid which fell down my back. I never wore makeup or wore my hair in a fancy style; Mom believed it was vanity if you spent too much time grooming yourself. Like Mom, I had shoulder-length, brown-colored hair, large brown eyes and a straight face. My skin was pale because I spent too much time indoors. This morning, I decided to wear a skirt with boots and a blouse. Nana Debby was praying in her room, I could hear her voice. She was seventy years old, but she was still strong and energetic. Mom's hair was always in a ponytail, she never wore makeup too.

Dad was mowing the lawn, the sound of the lawnmower thrummed in my ears as I walked into the living room. Mom was making breakfast; the aroma of food was in the air.

"Good morning, mom," I said.

"Good morning, Becky," She replied, "You'll run some errands for me this morning."

"Okay Mom," I replied, "Do you need any help now?"

"No," She replied, "After breakfast, you'll take some cookies to Miss Willow. She loves my cookies and I promised to send some to her today. You will also go to the bookstore and pick up some books for me."

Dad came into the kitchen, smelling of fresh grass. There was sweat on his brows, and he looked tired.

"Good morning, dad."

He nodded his head, opening the fridge to get a bottle of water. Dad was in his late fifties, but he was bald, so he looked older than his age. He had a moustache and dark eyes. Nana Debby came into the kitchen, wearing a red-colored dress which swept the floor as she walked. She had a shawl around her shoulders and a hat on her head.

"Mama, why are you dressed like this?" Mom asked, "Are you going somewhere this morning?"

"Good morning, nana," I said.

"Good morning, precious one," She said and then she turned to my mother, "I have a meeting with some women of virtue at the church."

Nana Debby had her own group which was made up of old ladies and the name of the group was women of virtue. I started setting the breakfast table while Dad went in to shower. He joined us some minutes later, we linked hands and Nana Debby said the grace. It was a taboo to talk during dinner, so we ate in silence, although, my parents talked when they had something important to say. Afterward, Mom offered to do the dishes, so I picked up the basket she had packed for Miss Willow and left the house. Miss Willow was a widow, she was in her fifties. She was a member of our church. She was also a nice lady and I liked her. She lived in a big, beautiful house in the town, she loved to bake; her pecan pie was the best in the town.

Rock of Roses was a beautiful town, the streets were neat, and the houses were quaint. Flowers, mostly roses were in everyone's garden, so the air always smelt fresh and clean. Miss Willow was on her porch, she smiled when she saw me. I waved at her as I walked up the porch.

"Good morning, ma'am."

"Morning, Becky," she said, pleasantly.

"My mother asked me to give this to you." I said, pointing at the basket.

Miss Willow's eyes lit up, the wrinkles around her lips creased as a huge smile appeared on her face.

"Thank you so much." She said, taking the basket from me, "Please tell her I appreciate her gift."

"I will," I smiled at her.

"Oh dear," She said, "What can I offer you?"

"I just had breakfast," I said, "Thank you."

She waved at me, "You are a special girl, Becky, and I hope you know that."

The smile on my face widened. I thanked her once again before I walked out of her yard. As I turned into the street where the bookshop was, someone yelled my name. It was Dave Spencer.

He had been asking me to be his girlfriend for years, but I always turned him down. Dave was twenty-three-years old, but he had no plans of going to college. My parents had decided that I would go to Bible college when I was done with college. I was schooling from home so I would be able to go to church regularly. Dave caught up with me, panting heavily. He looked so handsome, but I wasn't attracted to him because I knew that God had a better person for me. I wanted a man who would love me unconditionally and also love God. Dave wasn't a Christian; I had invited him to church several times, but he never came. My parents would be disappointed if they knew I was speaking to an unbeliever.

"Hey, Becks," He said.

"Hi,"

"Where are you heading to?"

"The bookshop," I replied.

"Sarah's getting married this weekend, will you be there?" He asked.

"No," I replied, "She didn't invite me to her wedding."

"Oh," He said, "Well, I don't have a date to the wedding. I was wondering if you'd like to go to the wedding with me as my date. I'll talk to Sarah; her boyfriend is my friend."

"Yeah, I know Jake is your friend." I replied, "I can't go to the wedding even if she invited me. However, if you want to see me again, you could come to church this Sunday."

"I can't come to the church this Sunday,"

"How about next Sunday?"

"I don't know yet." He replied.

"Alright, I guess I'll see you next Sunday. Have a nice day, Dave."

"You too," He replied.

Within minutes I was in the bookshop, apart from the church and the orphanage, I loved the bookshop. There were rows and rows of Christian books, devotionals, motivational and inspirational books. There were also Christian movies and songs. The interior of the bookshop was beautiful, the images of Jesus Christ were on the walls and there were beautiful floral wallpapers on the walls. The shop owner, Jackie Albert, a sweet middle-aged lady was behind the counter and as usual, she wore a smile on her face. Jackie was married, she had an identical twin boys. Today, she wore her red-colored hair in a bun, and she also wore a blue floral dress. Jackie had milky white skin with green eyes and spatters of freckles on her face.

"Hey, Becky, it's good to see you again." Jackie said.

"Hi Jackie, how are you?"

"I'm good," She smiled at me.

"I'm here to pick up some books for my mom." I said.

"We have some new collections, they are over there," she said, pointing in the direction of a brown-colored shelf. "Please let me know if you need my help."

"Thanks."

I found the books Mom wanted and I also bought a few devotionals that caught my attention. I didn't want to run into Dave again, so I went back home through another route, it was longer, but I wasn't in a hurry to get back home. Dad's car wasn't in the driveway but there was another car next to Mom's car. The car belonged to her friend, Molly. Aunt Molly was my mom's best friend and the only close friend she had. Molly had platinum blonde hair, tanned skin and grey eyes. She lived in the next town with her husband, so she rarely visited us. Mom often spoke to her on the phone, I don't know what they talked about, but they usually talked for a long time. Mom and Molly were in the kitchen, they were talking in hushed tones, and I was curious about their conversation. I moved closer to the kitchen door and stood beside the wall.

"I don't know what to do," Mom said, "My husband and I have grown apart. We rarely talk now."

I had no idea Mom and Dad was having problems in their relationship. They always seemed so perfect to me. I felt like walking away, but I wanted to know more, maybe I could find a way to help my parents.

"Why do you think your relationship isn't how it used to be?" Molly asked.

Mom sighed, "Sex, we don't have sex anymore."

Sex, oh my god, I have never heard Mom say that word. My cheeks became warm.

"Why don't you have sex anymore?" Molly asked, "Sex is enjoyable when both partners want it, especially when you introduce some toys into your sex life."

"Toys?" Mom asked, "Are you talking about adult sexual toys?"

"Of course, there is nothing wrong with using a sex toy with your partner."

Mom groaned, "We are Christians! Isn't it a sin?"

"No, it isn't a sin when you use a sex toy with your partner," Molly said, "Have you ever used a sex toy before? Alone?"

"What do you mean by alone?" Mom asked.

"Have you ever used a toy on yourself?" Molly asked, "Don't you ever touch yourself? Have you ever given yourself an orgasm?"

"My goodness," Mom cried, "No! I think it's a competition when you use a sex toy! Men are created for that purpose; you are supposed to make love to a man and not a toy."

My heart pounded with excitement. I was twenty-two-years-old, and I was still a virgin. I never touched myself or used a sex toy.

I didn't even know what a sex toy looked like. I knew there were toys that some women used for sexual pleasures, but I had never seen one before.

Molly laughed, "A sex toy should never be

viewed as competition. I got my first vibrator when I was twenty-two; I got it from my partner."

Mom's eyes widened, "Really?"

"Yes," Molly replied, "He wanted to try new things, but I was a little shy to use it with him due to my Christian upbringing. I also felt that it was a taboo. Anyway, I took the toy from him and took it home. One night, I tried it and I had the most amazing orgasm ever. When my partner gave me the toy, I acted like I didn't want it, but I used it every day. And yet I didn't start using sex toys with a partner until I was twenty-six-years old. Letting someone else in on my solo sex routine felt almost like peeing with them in the bathroom (which I've also done, to be honest, so I'm not sure why this was a big deal) after all he was the one who proposed it to me in the first place. But for some reason I felt guilty that I was the only one who was enjoying it. And I felt sorry for him because I couldn't experience orgasm with him just by having sex. No matter how long he made love to me, I never had an orgasm, so I kept it to myself. It took me four whole years before I finally confessed to him." Molly leaned against the wall, her voice had become emotional, "I thought he was going to make me feel like shit for not letting him know.

He looked at me and said, 'you actually thought after all those years I didn't catch up to your act?' So, we decide to use the sex toy together, to spice things up in the bedroom.

Oh my god, sex never felt so good before. For the first time in my life, I had an orgasm with him. It was so intense, and my toes curled up. Now that I've experienced the joys of simultaneous orgasms, I ain't ever going back. I'm a total sex toy evangelist. And I would not dare doing that without my partner and since then, he's used a few different products he'd never even heard of, let alone tried. And so, have I. Using lube alone opened up a lot of new sensations (and helped us go a lot longer without anything chafing), and every toy we've acquired has added fun and variety to our routine."

My jaw slackened as beads of perspiration formed on my forehead. Could sex toys be that good?

Nana Debby always rang it in my ear that masturbating was a terrible thing to do. How would my family react if they knew that I was considering using sex toys? Lord, save me. Molly went on, "First, let me say I would never want anyone to feel ashamed about how they do or don't orgasm. Climaxing during sex with your partner isn't always possible. That's why most couples incorporate foreplay into their love making. Anyway, I was always curious about what it would feel like to orgasm with my partner inside me or at the same time with him. I always imagined that it would be magical. However, I couldn't reach that sexual height with my partner until we started using sex toys together. I love how sex toys strengthened our bond. Sex with a toy is something every couple should try, at least, once in a while.

It gave us the opportunity to take care of each other at the same time. For the first time in years, my partner and I were able to climax at the same time-it was a beautiful experience. We often hear that most women can't achieve orgasm from sexual intercourse alone. If you can't achieve orgasm through sex, why not seek for help?

We should never be afraid to ask for help when we need it. If you can only climax while using sex toys, that's fine too, it doesn't make you a weirdo. So many people believe that men who can't satisfy their wives are the ones who use a sex toy on their women. Using a sex toy doesn't mean that your partner isn't a good lover. There are so many misconceptions about using sex toys, we need to be enlightened. ***Sex toys can't replace your partner***. Do you also know that sex toys have so many benefits? If things are becoming boring in your relationship, the answer is sex toys. Sex toys can add so many colors and excitement to your relationship. Sex toys can take you and your partner on an adventure. Things can become so exciting if you use sex toys. Sometimes, our relationship may not work out, but even that is a good experience. Despite all the positive and health benefits associated with sex toys, there is still a taboo about it. The best way to overcome the fear of using sex toys is to be open to your partner about it. If we can all discuss our sexual preferences with our partners, we will begin to see the use of sex toys as normal."

"How do I talk to my husband about this?" Mom asked, "I really want to spice things up in the bedroom, but I don't know how to. All we do now is to read the Bible together every night, then he would turn off the lights and we would go to bed."

"What do you want?" Molly asked, "Do you want to put some spark in your relationship? Do you want to be happy again in your marriage?"

"Yes, I want to be happy," She replied.

"Have you ever had a solo sex, and have you ever given yourself an orgasm?"

"No," Mom replied.

"How do you expect your husband to master your body when you haven't mastered your body? Which part of your body is the most sensitive?"

"I don't know." Mom said.

"Sex toys also have some health benefits," Molly said.

"They do?" Mom asked, there was surprise in her voice, "How can I get one?"

"I'll order something online and send it to you." Molly said. "If you enjoy using it, you can introduce it to your husband. Please explain to him that you are not trying to replace him, but you are only trying to be adventurous in the bedroom."

I had heard enough, my skin tingled as I tiptoed out of the house. Then I opened the door again, making so much noise so they would think that I just came in. Aunt Molly gave me a warm hug when she saw me. Mom had a worried expression on her face, but she smiled when she saw me. I gave Mom the books she asked me to pick up and then I fled into my bedroom.

Chapter III

My First Sex Toy

All through the week, I thought about the conversation I had overheard. I was still stunned that the quiet and lovely Aunt Molly used sex toys. My cheeks burned with embarrassment whenever I imagined using a sex toy. There were so many questions on my mind. I wondered if Mom would truly get a sex toy and use it. The idea of using a sex toy seemed so taboo. I also wondered what my family and church members would think of me if they found out that I had used or was using a sex toy. I didn't want to be punished by God too, but the idea was so tempting. It was all I thought of. I dreamt of sex toys and wished that I could use them. My stomach fluttered and tightened whenever I thought of sex toys. I started researching about sex toys online, I was surprised that several women all over the world used it; some women used it with their partners while some girls got sex toys as a present from their mom or boyfriend. I started fantasizing about owning a sex toy. I felt a feverish sensation in my body whenever I was alone. I wasn't feeling sick; I was just excited. Owning and using a sex toy has so many health benefits. There are also different types of sex toys; I blushed so hard when the image of the toys popped up while I was reading an article on a website. Instead of reading a devotional, I read an article about sex toys every day. I learned so much about sex toys and sex. Using a sex toy with your partner allows you to have greater and a more intense orgasm. It also improves sex life and self-confidence. The more a person uses a sex toy, the more they'll understand their body. I learned that when you explore your body and try out toys, you will know more about your body, and you will also get to know every erogenous spot on your body. The more you masturbate, the more you'll understand your body's need. Sex toys will make you feel relax and help you sleep better. It is also a fact that couples who incorporate sex toys into their sexual life are likely to have a lasting relationship than couples who do not use sex toys together. I also came across another article which says that every adult should have a sex toy because of its numeral benefits. Sex toys are great gadgets to have in the house because they are fantastic. The article also says that everyone should be proud of owning a sex toy. I wanted to have a sex toy too, I was twenty-two-years old, and I was legally old enough to own one. But my Christian upbringing stopped me from purchasing one. I tried not to think of sex toys, but I couldn't stop thinking about them. I was also dying to talk to someone about it. I couldn't contain my thoughts anymore. I had to share them with someone, anyone. So, I got a diary and started writing in it. At first, I filled the diary with my secret thoughts and desires. Then I decided it was time to do something about those thoughts running through my mind. All I needed was some confidence, a little boost. Whenever I read my diary, I was filled with an immense courage. But that courage deserted me each time I walked out through the door. However, the courage to own a sex toy finally came to me but in an unusual way. One Saturday morning, I went for choir rehearsal in the church. We had a rehearsal every Saturday, but Miss Brenda didn't show up. She was the lead singer. She was friendly with everyone, and she was always on time. We were all worried about her, I pulled out my phone from my pocket and dialed her number, but it went to her voicemail. After several attempts, I left a message for her. Some of the choir members suggested that we carry on without her, but I thought we should wait for her. She worked hard to write the song we would perform on Sunday. It would be unfair to her if we sang the song, she wrote without her. While we were still arguing, John, one of the backup singers came into the church with a worried expression on his face. We all rushed to him, throwing questions at him.

"Where is she?"
"Is she still coming?"

"When will she be here?"

John kept trying to say something, but he was interrupted each time.

Finally, it seemed as if he had enough because he yelled at us. Then another round of argument broke out. The older people in the choir seemed offended that he yelled to call them to order. I had to ensure that everyone was calm and then John apologized to everyone.

"I'm so sorry," John said, "I've been trying to talk, but no one gave me a chance to."

"We are sorry, John," I replied, "What is the problem? Where is Miss Brenda?"

"Yes, where is she?" Someone else asked.

"I have some news, but it is bad news." He said, "Miss Brenda is in the hospital, she had a heart attack last night."

"Oh my god," I cried, "How is she?"

"She will be alright, I guess," John said, "We'll have to rehearse the song without her. Who wants to be the new lead singer?"

A blonde-haired girl named Abby volunteered to be the lead singer. She was also a good singer, but she had a nasty attitude. She was a snob because her father was a senator. Also, she wasn't everyone's favorite. We all loved Miss Brenda and her angelic voice. All through the choir practice, I thought about Miss Brenda who always seemed so strong to me. She was one of the few women I liked in the church. Last summer, she gave my mom some of her family's recipes and showed her where she could get the ingredients. I just couldn't stop thinking about Brenda.

She was in her early thirties, yet she had a cardiac arrest. Later that day, I visited Miss Brenda at the hospital.

I didn't like the smell of hospital rooms and halls. The smell of sickness and disinfectant always gave me a sickening sensation. Miss Brenda was happy to see me, but she looked like a shadow of her old self. Her nice, big grin was gone, replaced by a sad smile. Her lustrous red hair had become tangled and stuck to her head as if she just came in from the rain. She also looked pale, and her body was connected to so many machines and tubes. When she spoke, her voice sounded so sad that it brought tears to my eyes. It seemed like the pastor and his wife had been there because there was a bottle of oil beside her. She tried to lift her arm, but it flopped back onto the bed. I felt sorry for her.

"Rebecca," she said in a quiet voice. "You came to see me, thank you."

"You are welcome," I replied, "How are you?"

She smiled and a tear slipped down her cheek, "My heart failed me."

I didn't know what to say so I placed a kiss on her cheek "You'll be alright. We'll keep praying for you."

"Prayers," She laughed, "Thank you."

"When do you think they will discharge you?" I asked, "I want to visit you again."

She shook her head, "I don't know."

I held her hand and gave it a gentle squeeze. It seemed like there was so much she wanted to say but she didn't have the strength to say them or maybe the words were too painful to say.

"Have you eaten?" I asked.

"I don't want food." She replied, "I want a second chance."

"What are you talking about?" I asked. "Of course, you'll get a second chance."

"I've realized that I haven't lived at all." She said, sobbing softly, "I regret not living my life when I had the chance. Society expected me to be a good girl and live my life by other people's expectations. I know you are like me, Rebecca. You are a good girl but being a good girl shouldn't stop you from doing the things you want. Don't live your life by people's expectations."

Her words made my heart squeeze. She placed a hand on mine, staring into my eyes. She smiled through her tears.

"Being a good girl sucks right?"

Tears rushed down my cheeks, but I couldn't help laughing, "Yes, it does."

"Life goes on, it doesn't wait for anyone." Brenda said, "Live your life every second of the day. Do the things you want, go to the places you want to go and even if you happen to break a few hearts, the good Lord will forgive you."

I sighed. "Brenda, do you want me to pray for you?"

"I have never tasted wine or champagne," She said, "I have never lived. I was waiting for my Mr. Right but it's a Mrs. Right, I want."

It took a few minutes before her words sank in; she wanted a Mrs. Right. Miss Brenda was into women; she was a lesbian, but I guess she kept herself pure because it was what was expected of her.

"Is there someone you like?" I asked.

She closed her eyes; tears clung to her long, dark lashes, "Yes."

"Where is she? Who is she?" I asked. "I will speak to her for you."

"It's too late." She replied, "She married someone else, a man. But she doesn't love him. I know she doesn't love him because of the way she looks at me. Why do we do this to ourselves?"

I didn't know what to say to her, but I felt so sorry for her. There was a look of regret in her eyes when she opened them. I kissed her cheek and promised to check up on her the next day. Miss Brenda passed away the next morning; her death threw everyone into mourning. She was loved by everyone. They held a vigil for her in the church and everyone came out to say something nice about her. When it was my turn, I said that she gave me the courage which I never had. There was a time that Miss Brenda was younger, every second of the day she had the chance to do what she wanted, but she didn't. Why? Because society was against it. Even as an adult, she could have walked into any grocery store to get a good wine and enjoy it in her room. She could have lived every day of her life, but she didn't. Yes, she did some great things, she wrote songs which we sang in the church. She was kind to everyone. Someone came out to say Miss Brenda used to babysit her kids every Saturday for free so she and her husband could go on a date. She helped everyone and was nice to everyone. But she never remembered herself. She never put herself first, not even once, because if she had, she would have realized that her life mattered too. I kept remembering her words and the regret in her voice. I dreamt about her at night, she looked happy, but it always seemed like she was trying to reach out to someone, but she couldn't. Her funeral was held on a rainy morning. Her parents were there, they cried so much. At that moment, I knew if the Lord returned their daughter to them, but he gave them the condition that they would allow her to marry the woman she loves, they would have accepted. Everyone from the church was at the funeral. They sang beautiful hymns most of which she had written. The pastor always said Miss Brenda was indispensable because of her talent, but someone had already taken her place before she was even laid to rest. Within a short time, I had realized some important things about life; YOU COME FIRST. During the funeral, I noticed that Jackie, the bookshop owner stood afar, sobbing. She looked so heartbroken. I gave her some minutes to pull herself together before I approached her. I had never seen Jackie so emotional. I didn't even know she was close to Miss Brenda. But the way she was sobbing, the way she placed her hand on her stomach, doubling over with pain showed that she genuinely cared about the deceased. When I got closer to her, she embraced me, sobbing so hard. It seemed like all she needed at that moment was a shoulder to lean on. Her husband and sons weren't at the funeral.

"Miss Brenda left so soon," I said.

"Yes, she was so young," Jackie replied.

"She was a lovely person." I said.

"Yes, the sweetest soul I know." Jackie replied, "And she had the most beautiful smile I had ever seen. I wish things had turned out differently for us."

My throat felt hot when I realized Jackie Albert was the woman Brenda had fallen in love with. I also realized that Jackie loved Brenda.

"She….um…. loved you," I said.

She looked alarmed but she relaxed when she saw the smile on my face. She nodded her head. I had also been living my life based on people's standard and expectations. I vowed to myself that I would start living my life the way I wanted it.

I yearned to own a sex toy and experiment with it. At that moment, I was determined to get a sex toy.

"Everyone is still here; do you want to leave now?" I asked.

"Yes," She replied.

We went back to the bookshop, but I didn't want to leave her alone. I stayed with her until evening, making small talk. Then her husband walked in with her boys. The children ran into her arms, hugging her. The boys started telling her about their day while she listened with so much love in her eyes. It was obvious that she loved her sons. But when she looked at her husband, the look in her eyes wasn't so fierce. I slipped out of the shop, but she looked up and mouthed the words, "thank you,"

I was sad as I walked back home. So many people aren't living their best lives because they are afraid of what others will say about them. When my house came into view, I didn't feel like it was home anymore. A home should be a place where you feel safe. A home shouldn't be a place where you are judged and criticized for wanting to be you. But I didn't have the courage to leave; after all, I was a good girl. I was my mother's daughter.

Consumed by a burning desire to own a sex toy, I started surfing the internet. I went on so many adult websites, giggling as I put various toys into my cart. However, it dawned on me that my family could get suspicious if I had so many packages delivered to the house. So, I removed all the toys in the cart, except for a vibrator which I paid for. I was excited when I became the proud owner of a vibrator, but another huddle was how to get the package without the knowledge of my family. I was bold enough to purchase a vibrator online, but I wasn't bold enough to give them the correct address. So, I gave them the community hall's address. I waited at the community hall on the day I was supposed to receive the package.

The deliveryman didn't say anything even though it was obvious that I gave him the wrong address.

"Take care, Miss," he said.

"Thank you." I replied.

I cradled the package as I walked home briskly. Nana Debby and Mom were at a fundraiser while Dad was at work. My heart pounded with excitement as I looked at my first sex toy. The vibrator was made of silicone, and it had a purple color. It had a slim penis with a tiny penis head.

I took off my clothes, blushing as I slid under the bed covers. I took the vibrator into my mouth and suckled it. I had watched some soft pornography on the internet, so I had a little idea of how to suck a cock. I licked the sides and swirled my tongue around the crown. I moaned out as I used my hands to tease my nipples. I was becoming aroused. My pussy pulsated, sending electrical currents through my veins. I licked my lips, moaning as my body shook.

I switched on the vibrator and a humming sound filled the room. My heart hammered against my chest, my fingers were trembling, and my palms felt so clammy. The vibrator slipped out of my hands several times because I was nervous. I placed the tip of the vibrator on my nipples, and they began to harden. I was stunned. My nipples started to tingle as I brushed the tip of the vibrator over them. My stomach knotted as a sweet pleasure washed over me. My vagina moistened. I learned online that vagina was also called pussy, kitty or cunt.

I slid my hands over my body, caressing my skin as I brushed the tip of the vibrator over my breasts. My fingers mistakenly increased the speed level of the vibrator. A moan tumbled out of my lips. My pussy lips quivered as a slimy fluid trickled down my thighs. I placed the vibrator on my clitoris; I sucked in air as a wave of pleasure washed over me. I pressed the vibrator against my pussy lips, my abdomen clenched hard as a tremor ran through me. My clitoral hood stretched as sensations rippled through me. I pushed the tip of the vibrator into my tight, virgin pussy.

"Awww…" I cried.

I started to convulse as a flood of pleasure engulfed my body. My clitoris throbbed painfully. I rubbed my fingers over my clit, brushing my fingers over it, back and forth. I had another orgasm. Tears rushed down my cheeks. I wanted to give myself another orgasm, but I was tired. So, I stroked the toy with my tongue, licking it until it was clean. Then I put the tip into my mouth, just sucking on it.

I felt a little guilty, but I also felt relaxed. I put the toy between my legs, scooped my juice onto it and put it into my mouth. I did this several times. I cradled my first sex toy in my hand, wondering if it would be the only toy I would have. A part of me already knew I wouldn't be satisfied with just one toy. But how would I get another toy and conceal it without anyone knowing?

JIRO CHATELAIN

Chapter IV

Trying out Anal Beads

It was a happy day for me when I woke up; I felt like I won the jackpot. There was a huge smile on my face as my eyes greeted the rays of the sunlight. My body felt so relaxed, and I smiled to myself whenever I remembered the massive orgasm, I had given myself. When I went downstairs, everyone was surprised by the happy look on my face. Nana wanted to know the secret behind my smile. I had played with my sex toy all through the night. I had also given myself multiple orgasms. I was convinced that I needed more sex toys, but I didn't know which one to get. Shopping for sex toys could be thrilling and also confusing. There are so many toys out there, you'd wonder if the one you are choosing is the best for you. But I had made up my mind to always buy whatever toy caught my fancy.

"Rebecca, you look so relaxed," Mom commented.

"Thanks, Mom." I replied.

"What happened to you," Nana said, staring at me, "You look so different, and so happy."

I laughed as I poured cereal into a cereal bowl, "I always look happy, don't I?"

"What we are trying to say is that you are glowing this morning," Mom said, "Did you sleep well last night?"

"Yes, I did," I replied.

Mom sighed, "I couldn't sleep yet my body feels so tired."

"You need to share your secret with us, girl," Nana joked.

"There is no secret to share," I replied, sitting at the table.

"I guess it's the Lord's doing," Nana said, "The good Lord always takes care of his own."

"Yes, he does," I replied.

After breakfast, I rushed back into my room to prepare for school. Dad dropped me off at school, he didn't comment about my happy mood, but he was curious. I had a class every morning, but this morning seemed different because my brain was functioning greatly. I answered almost all the questions the professor asked. I also enjoyed the class because my mind was at peace. After class, I didn't rush to leave.

Instead, I approached the professor, Miss Daniels, to ask her some questions. She seemed surprised that I came up to her to ask her questions. But she answered my questions. As I walked out of the classroom, I saw a group of girls standing in the corridor. Some of them were familiar faces but I didn't know their names. The popular girls often avoided girls like me who don't party and smoke. I overheard their discussion, so I slowed the paced of my footsteps.

"I have herpes." One girl said.

"You should stop sleeping around," Another girl said. "A week ago, you had STD and now you have herpes?"

"I can't help it," The first girl said, "I feel so horny all the time; my stupid boyfriend wouldn't stop sleeping around too. My life is a big mess."

"Then, you should get a dildo or something." The second girl said, "Don't you have a collection of sex toys you can use whenever you are horny? One of the benefits of using a sex toy is that you won't be at risk of contracting sexual diseases. But you should clean all your toys after using them."

The girls laughed.

"I'm going to the hospital tomorrow."
The first girl said, "I don't know what to do,
how will I take care of my sexual needs and
urges."

They all burst into laughter. I pretended as if I
was busy with my phone, but I was only there
because I was enjoying their conversations. I
didn't want to introduce myself to them or
make friends with them. But I was curious to
know more about sex toys.

"You need sex toys," The second girl said
again, "I got my first sex toy when I was
sixteen. Then my mom took me to the
hospital and my doctor put me on the pills.
The sex toy was a gift from my mom. She
knew that girls my age were already having
sex with boys at the back of their trucks. But

she wanted me to have a better sexual life. Listen, most of those girls got pregnant and couldn't go to college. One of them had HIV. My mom asked me to play with the sex toy; she said it would help me have a better idea about a boy's genital. If you can please yourself, no boy can say nasty things about your body or make you feel insecure."

"What happened after you used the toy?" The first girl asked.

"Well, I enjoyed it, but I didn't break my hymen," The second girl replied, "I realized that I wasn't ready to have sex with any boy. I just wanted to give myself an orgasm whenever I had the urge. Four years later, I was still a virgin, but I had known so much about my body.

Then I met a boy who I liked, and we had sex. The sex was great, it was really amazing."

The girls laughed.

"We broke up when I got into college, but we are still friends," The second girl went on, "If my mom hadn't introduced me to sex toys, I would have given my body to a random boy who wouldn't appreciate it. I am still on the pills, but I won't let you fuck me if you can't give me an orgasm. My sex toys have set the standards so high, if you wanna get down with me, you must be ready to give me some pleasure too."

A red-haired girl whose name was Sandy clapped her hands.

"That's awesome," She said, "My parents use sex toys,"

"For real?" The girls asked, laughing.

"Yeah, and they have been married for thirty years," Sandy said, "They don't hide their toys and they are not ashamed about it. My dad travels a lot, he brings back a new sex toy for my mom each he went on a trip. He says he wouldn't feel comfortable if she didn't have any sex toys to play with when he isn't around. He also travels with some sex toys which he uses over there. My folks are weird, their lifestyle embarrasses me sometimes, but they are so much in love with each other."

I was intrigued by what Sandy said. If only couples could use sex toys together, they would have so much fun.

"I started using sex toys when I was eighteen," Sandy said, "Now I have collection of toys. I love my toys and I never go anywhere without them." She slipped out a small lipstick-sized sex toy out of her purse. "I even bought some anal beads last week,"

The girls started to talk at once, they were all excited. Why didn't I think of anal beads before? I wanted to try them too and see if they are as good as vibrators. I slipped out my phone and I found some articles on anal beads. I went to my next class and left for home after the class. I ordered some anal beads online; the deliveryman was waiting for me by the time I got to the town hall. He handed the package to me and within minutes I was in my bedroom.

I washed my butthole in the bathroom; it felt good to feel the jets of the water against my anal rim. I dipped a finger into my anal cavity and ensured that the residue of goo was out of me. I dried my ass cheeks with a clean towel and then I went back into the bedroom.

Anal beads have some health benefits too, if you are scared of falling pregnant, you can safely use an anal bead s to achieve orgasm. It allows you to have a powerful, stronger and intense orgasm. I licked the beads, making them wet with my tongue. I pulled and squeezed my breasts as I played with the beads.

"Mmmm…"

I spread my legs apart, rubbing a bead over my clit. My sensitive clit hardened when I skimmed the bead over the top. I slipped a finger into my hot pussy, rubbing the front wall of my pussy with my finger. My body was on fire. My rectum was already leaking juice. I rubbed a finger around my butthole and the most amazing feeling washed over me. My body arched, my toes curled up and my pussy shot out some juice. I thrust a finger into my butthole, moaning as adrenaline pumped through my veins. Anal orgasm is so different from the orgasm you achieve when you play with your pussy or clit. I thrust a finger into my pussy while digging another finger into my butthole. I pulled out both fingers and sniffed them. Closing my eyes, I shoved both fingers into my mouth, sucking my musky juice off them.

My clit twitched. My nipples were rock hard.

I never knew that I could pleasure myself and still remain a virgin. While playing with my butthole, I realized how sensitive my anal rim was. I slipped two fingers into my butthole; a burning sensation washed over me. My butthole felt so full, it throbbed a little and it also stung when I touched it. I started to fuck my butthole with my fingers while fondling my breasts. I picked up two anal beads, rubbed them around my anal ring until they were coated in my thick, gooey fluid. The beads popped into my ass, stretching my rectum.

I pounded my fists on the bed, moaning. I had an instant orgasm. I groaned when the anal bead slipped into my anal cavity. More juice leaked out of me. I pinched my clit, rubbing my pussy lips. My stomach knotted as I had another climax. I was struggling to breathe; my breath was coming out in pants and my juice was running down my legs.

Chapter V

My Body Is Mine

My home was unusually quiet, something was going on that I didn't know about. There was some tension in the house, it was so thick. I could feel it; no one spoke during dinner or breakfast. At first, I wondered if God was punishing my family because I had started using sex toys. However, I laughed when I realized how ridiculous that thought was. Dad rarely came home now; maybe he was busy with church or something else. Mom always kept to herself. She attended prayer vigil every night. She did charity works every week and sometimes she starved herself. She wouldn't talk to anyone about her problems. I thought my parents had a fight, but it was worse; they were growing apart every day. Sometimes it seemed like they were avoiding each other. If Dad was in the house, Mom would be at church. It seemed like they had unconsciously planned it so they wouldn't be in the same place, at the same time. Nana and I dined alone on some nights because Mom didn't have an appetite.

I helped with the chores so Mom could rest, but she still continued to clean and do house chores obsessively. She would clean spots that were already clean, wipe imaginary dust away from the sofa and sweep the floors every second. If she wasn't cooking or cleaning, she would be inside her room, praying or reading the Bible. One day after lunch, Nana wanted to take a walk. Mom was humming a sad song as she cleaned the kitchen tiles for the umpteenth time. I wished I could help her, but she didn't want anyone's help. She would push my hands away if I tried to take the washcloth away from her. Mom's fingernails looked old and discolored because she was always putting them in water. Her skin had lost its shine. Some nights, I heard her crying in her bedroom, usually on the nights Dad decided to go for prayer vigils alone.

I didn't know what to do, so I took my shawl and went after Nana. The sun was already making its way back home, casting a beautiful, colorful glow in the sky. The evening breeze felt cool on our faces, and we could perceive the wonderful fragrance of the wildflowers in the environment. Nana sang as we walked through the street, it was a beautiful, old song about God's love. Her song warmed my heart, reminding me of God's love.

"Nana, why is there so much sadness in our home?" I asked. "Can you feel it? I feel like I have to walk on eggshells around Mom. She isn't living a healthy life. She keeps cleaning and making so much food, yet she wouldn't have any of it."

"I pray the good Lord shines His light on our home," Nana said, "There comes a time that life's problems weigh us down and we can't do anything. No matter how hard we try to help ourselves; only God's love can save us."

"What's going on with Dad?" I asked, "He now finds a reason to stay out late,"

Nana laughed, "I don't know. I am praying for your parents."

"Why won't Mom speak to anyone or ask for help?" I asked.

Nana sighed, "It's my fault. As a parent we try our best to help our children grow into independent adults. Your mother has always been told to be strong and to focus her attention on God. I wasn't a good mother, but I wasn't a bad mother either. I did my best to make her grow into a beautiful woman who loves and respects God. However, no matter how hard you try to train a child, they will always have their own personality. And when that child becomes an adult, you wouldn't be able to control the choices he or she makes. All you can do is counsel and pray for your child."

Nana had become tired, so we walked into a park and sat on one of the benches.

"Your aunt, the one who passed away when you were a baby…" Nana said, "I don't like to talk about her."

Mom had a younger sister who passed away when I was born. But Mom always acted as if she was an only child.

"What happened to her?"

"I made her marry a man she wasn't in love with," Nana said, her voice was filled with regrets; "Mary wasn't as quiet as your mother. She always had a mind of her own, but I wanted her to marry right. I wanted her to marry the man God had destined for her. But I made a fatal mistake, I tried to play God's role. A young pastor, Jonas, was transferred to our church. I liked him, he seemed like a decent man, and I believed he was God's anointed. One day, he told me the Lord revealed it to him that Mary was his wife. I was happy. I didn't pray about it, I forced Mary to marry him. I cried and manipulated her; I have regretted it since then."

"What happened?" I asked.

"They got married, but he physically abused her for years until she couldn't take it anymore." Nana said, "I didn't know about the abuse, she didn't tell anyone. How could she? She felt betrayed. The first time I noticed a bruise on her arm was at your parents' wedding. I didn't want to ruin your Mother's Day because they were best friends. They loved each other dearly. When you were born, Mary decided she wanted to leave but he wouldn't let her leave. Jonas murdered her and threw her body into a lake to make it seem like she drowned. Then he went back home and shot himself. We moved away from the town, but we were never the same again. Even when your grandfather was on his deathbed, he blamed me for Mary's death."

"I am sorry, Nana," I said, "You couldn't have known Jonas was a horrible man. Why do you keep going to church? Doesn't it bring back unpleasant memories?"

"I knew the devil was trying to test my faith," Nana said, "If I stopped worshiping God, then it means the devil has won."

We remained quiet for a while but there was another question on my mind.

"Nana," I called.

She turned to look at me, "What's on your mind, child?"

My throat was suddenly dry. I swallowed hard as I struggled to get the words to roll off my chest.

"Why is there an increase in divorce amongst Christian women?" I asked,

"Divorce is a sin, yet there are some many broken Christian homes."

The wrinkles around her lips stretched as she smiled. She held my hand. Nana's fingers were so bony. She sighed as she looked at the sky.

"Yes, divorce is a sin but if it will cost you your life, I will advise you to leave." She replied. "Another reason for high divorce rate amongst Christians is that so many women misunderstand the teachings of the Bible. Also, some pastors misinterpret the Bible, leading their congregations to commit more sin. When I was a young girl, we were raised to love the Lord and obey His commandments. We were taught to read the Bible and show love to everyone around us.

The problem is that these days many women worship their pastors instead of the Lord. They show more respect to their pastors and spiritual leaders than they do their husbands."

"Nana, is that the reason many Christian homes are falling apart?"

"There are so many reasons for a divorce," Nana said, "People divorce because they lost interest in their partner. If one partner becomes abusive, lazy or even stops grooming him or herself, there will be a problem in the marriage."

"Oh," I said.

"Have you taken a look at your mother lately?" Nana asked.

"Well, I see her every day; she doesn't look different to me."

"She looks like a maid, not a wife," Nana said.

"Nana!" I cried.

"It's the truth, my child." Nana said, "Husbands wants their wives to look like wives and not maids. She wears those drab gowns with granny panties."

My face felt hot, I was shocked. I had never heard Nana speak so frankly before.

"Well, that's true."

"Rebecca, being a Christian doesn't mean you have to neglect your wifely duties." Nana said, "You have to look good for your husband, make him desire you even if he is miles away from you. A woman should wear good perfumes and nice lingerie. I know you've never heard me speak like this, but many women have abandoned their wifely duties, forgetting that their husbands are humans."

"Nobody has ever talked to me about these things." I said.

"We didn't want you to have any wild idea." Nana said, "Your body is the temple of the lord, but do you know what? It is also yours and you have to protect it."

"My body is mine," I whispered.

"Yes, it's all yours." Nana said. "When your grandfather was still alive and your mother was still a child, we used to sneak into the basement to make love. Sometimes he would wake me up with kisses; we would go into the bathroom and have a nice time. I was a Christian wife, but I never wore old, dirty lingerie or looked like an old maid. Sometimes on our way from church, your grandfather would signal to me to meet him in the woods. We would tell the nanny to go home with the kids."

I giggled. "Nana, I thought these things are sinful acts."

"When you are legally married, no act of love making is a sin as long as you both consent to it." Nana said, "The good Lord made woman for man because He didn't want him to be alone, but these days, many married women and men are still lonely. They never talk about anything except the happenings in the church. They have no life outside the church. All they do is make babies, go to church and hope to make heaven someday."

She placed her hand on mine.

"Thank you for sharing this with me, Nana,"

"You should remember that you have to be your husband's best friend." She said, "What do best friends do?"

"Ummm…"

"Best friends have fun together, they fight and make up," Nana said, "They go on adventures, and they always have each other's back."

Nana's words rang in my ears as I lay in bed that night. My body is mine. I have to protect it. There are several ways to protect our body, eating healthy, exercising and not having unprotected sex. I wanted to be good to my body. I wanted to go on adventures with my body and give it so much pleasure. I wanted to discover every secret sensitive spot on my skin. I placed my hand on my pussy, it was hairy. I went into the bathroom and shaved off the hair on my mound with a razor. I was careful; there wasn't a single cut on my mound when I was done. I washed my pussy with warm water and then ran a towel over it. I padded my way back into my bedroom. I was naked from the waist down. I stood in front of my full-length mirror, admiring my shaven pussy. It was the first time I was actually seeing my pussy. I always thought it was a sin to touch myself or look at my pussy. My body tingled as I looked at the reflection of my pussy. It looked like a lovely flower with puffy petals, a pink bud and milky nectar. I sat on the bed, facing the mirror. I spread my legs apart, staring at the beautiful pink valley between my pussy lips. My clit became erect. I was fascinated.

Tears filled my eyes, spilling down my cheeks. My body was mine since I was born but I had never explored it. I had never taken a look at my body to appreciate it. I noticed how my abdomen bulged slightly but my belly was flat. My breasts were round, and my nipples were perky. My hips were curved, my thighs were slender, and my legs were long. I held my pussy lips apart with my fingers, I plunged a finger into my pussy. I arched my back as a sweet, incredible sensation washed over me. Slowly, I worked my finger in and out of my pussy. I moaned out as pleasure exploded inside me. My finger brushed against a spongy tissue in the upper wall of my pussy. I pulled in a deep breath as my stomach tightened. A strong orgasm hit me. I closed my thighs, struggling against the wave of guilt that was trying to attack me.

I reached for my phone and ordered some new sex toys, a vibrating ring and a wearable wireless G-spot vibrator.

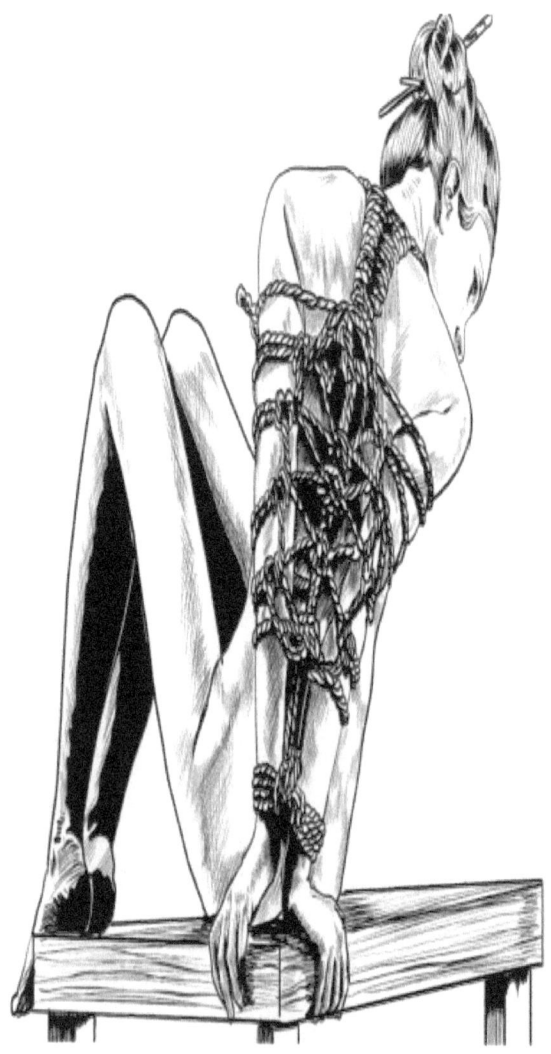

Chapter VI

Sex Toys Collector

The new set of sex toys I ordered came the following morning. I got a complimentary vibrating egg. Mom was in the kitchen when I got back home, cradling my prized sex toys in my arms. I didn't know if I had gone crazy or not, but I didn't want to hide my toys anymore. Using a sex toy isn't something to be ashamed of. Mom had her back to me when I walked in, she nodded to acknowledge my presence, but she didn't turn back. I went into my bedroom and closed the door. Then I pulled out a small box underneath my bed. My sex toy collection was growing. I wanted to explore all the toys that were in the world.

I slipped the pink vibrating ring onto my left finger. It fitted perfectly. It also looked beautiful on my finger. Instead of taking off my clothes, I slipped my hand into my panties. I pressed the knob that was on the ring against my clit.

"Awww,"

The feeling was heavenly. I rotated my finger against my clit. The ring vibrated against my clit, sending pulsating waves of pleasure through me. Spreading my legs apart, I pulled down my skirt and panties with one hand. I leaned against my window, feeling the cool breeze on my face. A thrill went through me; my nipples began to throb immediately. My excitement increased. I moaned out, so loudly that Mom could have heard me. My knees were weak. I pushed a hand into my blouse, lifting my bra up. I sighed when my fingers came in contact with my taut nipples. I rubbed my nipples, moaning as sparks of electricity went off inside me. I felt a little moisture between my legs, but it soon turned into a river. My juice rushed down my legs, I couldn't stop moaning. I took my phone, searched through the media file and played a classic country song. I started to sway to the song, closing my eyes. I imagined that I was on a beach. I perceived the smell of the sea, heard the song of the birds and heard the sound of the wind. My fantasy lover came out of the water, gloriously naked. He had a tanned, lean body.

He was tall, dark and sexy. He swirled me toward the sea until we were standing in the water. My skin felt so cool. He pressed a soft kiss against my lips. His tongue slipped into my warm mouth, exploring the depth of my mouth as he caressed my body. We lay in the water, the sand sticking to our backs. He caressed my breasts. He murmured hotly into my ears as he dragged his tongue down my wet, salty skin. He nibbled on my skin as his hands journeyed down my body. He stroked every inch of my skin as he pushed his rock-hard penis against my thighs. I sighed as I widened my thighs. He rubbed my pussy, stroking my wet valley with the pad of his fingers. He pushed my legs apart, placing his head between my thighs. He licked my pussy.

With my sex toys, I could go on a voyage without leaving my room. With my sex toys and my imagination, I could travel to any part of the world and be whatever I wanted to be.

The next toy I bought was a remote-controlled panty vibrator. The toy could be worn underneath any underwear. But the one I purchased came with a set of silky, sexy panties. I had never owned anything so sexy. I stood in front of the mirror, admiring my sexy butts. Then I tucked the toy into the panties before I stepped out of the house. I downloaded the remote control on my phone so I could use it in public. Then I wore a dress and a jacket. I had several errands to run but I'd never have a boring day again. I had orgasms throughout the day, one while I was in the church. I had another one while I was in a boring class. I had a smile on my face throughout the day and I also felt relaxed. By the time I got back home, my panties were sopped with my juice. I started to look up new sex toys on the internet. There are thousands of sex toys in the words but sadly, many people don't know that. I didn't feel insecure about my looks anymore because I realized that my body was perfect just the way it was. Sex toys will make one have a positive mindset about their bodies. I also realized that one can never have too many sex toys. If people used sex toys often their chances of contracting a sexually transmitted disease would be low because sex toys can't give you sexually transmitted diseases. After going through a collection of sex toys online,

I decided to buy a clit stimulator. The clitoris could give one an immense pleasure but unfortunately it doesn't get enough attention.

The tension in the house seemed to be growing every day. Nana was busy with her charity work, so I hardly saw her. Mom was always in the kitchen, either cooking or cleaning. Dad often stayed out late until midnight; sometimes we had dinner without him. I had been brought up not to interfere in whatever was going on between my parents. But I couldn't bear the deafening silence and sighs anymore. One evening, I knocked on my parents' door, Dad wasn't back yet but Mom was in the room. She opened the room; it was obvious that she had been crying.

"Mom, are you alright?" I asked.

"Yes," She replied, "What do you want?"

"I wanted to talk to you." I said.

"Oh, do you want to come in?" She asked.

We walked into the room together; she sat on the bed while I stood at the door.

"Mom,"

"What do you want to talk about?" She asked.

"It's about you and Dad, what's going on?"

"I'm handling the situation." She said, "We had a little fallout, but the Lord is in control."

"Mom, I think you and Dad need to see a counselor." I said.

Her eyes widened as she looked alarmed.

"Christians don't need marriage counselors." Mom replied, "I am praying about the situation. If my strength fails me, I will talk to Pastor Paul, and he will pray for me."

"It's not a sin to seek for help when you need it," I said.

"You are too young to understand how things work in the real world." She sighed.

"I am not too young, Mom, I am not a child anymore." I replied. "I want you to get help, you and Dad."

"Thanks, darling, but we will be fine." She said.

I walked out of the room with a heavy heart. As I lay in my bed with the clit stimulator between my thighs, all the sadness drained out of me. The clit stimulator sucked my clit, sending waves of pleasure through me. It pulled my clit back and forth, suctioning it. I had multiple waves of orgasm; I slept off with the toy between my legs.

Chapter VII

Masturbation Class

"Miss Willow, are you in?" I called, knocking on the door.

Swinging the basket in my hand, I walked into the yard, but she wasn't there either. However, I could hear the sound of laughter coming from the house. It was a Saturday morning; Mom had asked me to deliver a basket of baked goods to Miss Willow. I went around to the front of the door and knocked harder. The door opened and a lovely woman strolled out. She smiled at me; it was the most beautiful smile I had ever seen.

"Hello, sweetheart, are you here for the class?" She asked.

"Class?"

She opened the door wider, "Please come in."

"Umm…. I'm here to see Miss Willow, is she around?"

"I'm Alice," She said, "I am Willow's half-sister. Willow went on vacation, so I am house-sitting for her."

"Oh, I didn't know she traveled." I replied, "My mother asked me to give this basket to her. You can have it if you want, it contains baked goods."

Her lips curved into a smile, "That's sweet of you."

I gave her the basket and turned around, walking down the porch.

"Wait," She called.

I walked up the porch, back to her.

"What is your name?"

"I'm Rebecca Hayes."

"Would you like to join the class?" She asked, "Come in,"

I walked into the house with Alice. I gasped when I saw six naked women in the room. There were yoga mats on the floor; there were lubricant, a bottle of massage oil and sex toys beside each mat. The women didn't seem surprised to see me.

"I am a sex educator," Alice said, laughing. "These are my students, come forward my darlings and introduce yourself to your new classmate."

"I'm Sally," A blonde-haired woman said.

"I am Jessie," Another blonde said.

A dark-haired, skinny woman embraced me; her name was Emily. The other women were Aurora, Meg, and Audrey. The women gave me a warm welcome although I hadn't met anyone of them before. Most of them were from the neighboring towns.

"You can take off your clothes sweetie while I get another yoga mat for you." Alice said. Her voice was loud, but it held so much warmth.

My cheeks burned. "Where is the bathroom?"

Alice laughed, "Honey, you can take off your clothes here."

I had never taken my clothes off in front of anyone before.

"It's not so hard once you take off something," Emily said.

I pulled my blouse off and took off my bra. I felt a burning shame and I covered my breasts with my hands. The other women laughed.

"Your body is gorgeous," Alice said, "Why do you feel the need to cover it?"

Alice left the room, disappearing down a hallway. The other women settled on their mats while I took off my skirt and panties. Alice came back into the room with a pink-colored yoga mat for me. She laid the mat on the floor for me.

"Thank you," I said, sitting on the mat.

I chatted with the other women; they were easy to talk. It felt like I had known them for years. We talked about everything from the weather to their families and back to the class. They all had high praises for Alice. I wasn't nervous anymore, I was excited. Alice clapped her hands, smiling.

"Who is excited to be here?" Alice asked.

All hands went up, including mine.

Alice picked up a huge dildo, "This is a fake cock, but it has helped several women, especially to retain their sanity and keep their marriage." She laughed at her joke, even louder than we did. "Rebecca, this is the first class, so you haven't missed out on anything." She pointed at Meg, "Please come forward and tell us what you like about your body."

Meg shot to her feet, with a huge smile on her face. She wiggled her ass a bit which made us to laugh.

"Hi everyone," Meg said, breathlessly, "I am a mother of three. As you can see, there are several stretch marks and cellulite on my stomach. But I love my belly so much," She rubbed her hands over it, "This big tummy has carried three wonderful kids who are the center of my universe."

"Do you have a satisfactory sexual life?" Alice asked, "Are you happy about your orgasms?"

Meg shook her head, "I am not satisfied with my sex life. I fake orgasm most times. My husband doesn't know that I fake it, but I just can't achieve orgasm."

"Have you ever tried to give yourself an orgasm?" Alice asked.

"Yes, I have tried but I just can't get it right." Meg replied.

"Thank you." Alice said, "Aurora, come over here darling and tell us if your clit obeys you or not."

We all burst into laughter. Aurora stood beside Alice. I noticed that her hips were large, but her legs were slim. She had big labia with a long clit which looked like a tiny cock.

"My clit obeys me." Aurora said.

We all laughed again.

Alice clapped her hands, "Now darling, tell us what you like about your body and the best way you achieve orgasm."

Aurora grinned, "Five years ago, I had cancer of the breast; the right breast. It was a hard time for me because my fiancé dumped me when he found out. Apparently, he loved my boobs more than he loved me."

My gaze strayed to her breasts; she had the biggest breasts in the room. Her nipples were long and dusky.

"I started to hate my breasts and the pains it caused me." She went on. "I survived the cancer; fortunately, I didn't lose my breast. But I couldn't love my breasts anymore. It took me a long time before I could get over the hatred that I had for my breasts. I love my breasts now." She cupped her breasts, "My new boyfriend is so crazy about these girls,"

"Are you happy about your orgasms?" Alice asked.

"I am happy with my orgasms." She replied, "However, I'd like to squirt during orgasm."

Alice smiled, "Your clit is yours to command and it will obey you."

Next, Emily came out. She was slender, really skinny with no meat on her bones. She lifted her right leg, giving us a view of her pussy. Emily's pussy was shaved.

"I love my legs," She said, "It really turns me on when a man slides his hand down my thighs. As for orgasms, I have never had an orgasm."

Alice gasped, "You need to pet your kitty more."

Emily laughed. Sally stepped forward; she had a scar line along her abdomen. She was chubby, her stomach was big, and she had fleshy thighs. But she still looked so sexy.

"I hated my body since I was a teenager," Sally said, "I wanted to be a skinny girl. I went on several diets and sometimes I starved myself. However, I met someone who made me think differently about my body. I met my wife, Jasmine." A pretty smile appeared on her face, "Jasmine is slender and pretty. I thought she was out of my league. Yet, she didn't see the folds of fat around my stomach or under my chin. She fell in love with me, every day she holds me in her arms and tells me how much she loves my body. I love my body, every part of me. I love my fat stomach and fat ass."

We all laughed.

"You love your orgasms too?" Alice asked.

"Oh yes," Sally cried, "I love my orgasms. I am happy about my orgasms."

Jessie jumped to her feet, smiling from cheek to cheek. She looked beautiful too. At this point I had realized that every woman is beautiful just the way they are. Despite your body size or the way, you look, you are beautiful, and you are enough. Most times, we hate our body because we focus on all the flaws in our beautiful bodies. Each of the women was beautiful, yet they felt insecure about their body.

"Oh, me and my little body," Jessie said, laughing, "There is a misconception about body shaming. Most people don't know skinny women get body shamed too. In my family, everyone is on the plus size. I am the only skinny person in the family. My parents were worried that I might be anemic."

We all laughed. Jessie continued her narration when the noise lessened. "My mother always complained that I wasn't eating right, why? It was because I wasn't fat. My cousins verbally abused me, and body shamed me. They said nasty words to me at every chance they had. They made me hate my body. I wanted to put on some weight so they could just back off and leave me alone. I made myself sick by eating so much.

Damn, I didn't even want to look at myself in the mirror. Then I went online, seeking for help but there are limited articles about skinny women being body shamed. I decided to move out of the house, and I got my own place. Every day, I looked into the mirror, and I told myself that my body was beautiful. I told myself that God built the right body for me, he took his time to create me, and he loved me. It took a long time, but I started to feel better about my body. I love my skinny body, my lean waist and sexy legs." She twirled, shaking her little ass, "I love my little body. This body has given me the best orgasm ever."

We cheered her as she walked back to her position.

Alice clapped, "Rebecca, please come forward."

I stood up and graciously stood in front of them. Taking a deep breath, I began to tell them what I loved about my body.

"I love my body." I said, "I love every part of my body and it's all thanks to sex toys."

The women giggled.

"I haven't had sex because I am keeping myself for the right man." I continued, "However, I give myself amazing orgasms with the aid of my sex toys."

"That's it, girl!" Alice said.

The other women cheered, loudly.

"I love my orgasms; I am happy about my orgasms."

"Wow!" Meg cried.

Then Audrey came forward.

"I love my ass," She said, reaching behind her to squeeze her ass, "I love the way it bounces when I am riding on a hard cock."

Cheers, applause and laughter filled the air. Audrey bowed a little before she went on.

"My ass is so sensitive; I can feel thousands of vibrations run through it when I squeeze it. I've had so many orgasms and it was because of my ass."

Alice clapped her hands. "I love you all,"

"We love you too, Alice," We chorused.

"Orgasms have been a part of my life since I was a young girl." Alice said, "It was my answer to all of life's problems. I gave myself an orgasm for all my little achievements. I gave myself an orgasm when I had a problem, and I didn't know how to solve it. I gave myself orgasms for so many reasons, it's my body and it deserves to be pampered too. Many women give their men orgasms all the time, but they never remember to give themselves one."

All the women nodded their heads.

"Now, we are going to do another exercise." Alice said. "Everyone spread your legs apart."

We all pushed our legs apart.

"Look at your pussy,"

We all did.

"Your pussy is a garden." She said, "It's beautiful, the petals, the nectar and the colors around it. It's all breathtakingly beautiful. Has anyone ever taken a look at a garden and said what an ugly garden?"

"No," We all chorused.

"Look at each other's garden and compliment it." Alice said. "Rebecca, I love your vagina. It's so pretty."

I blushed. "Thank you."

"I love your clit; it looks so pink and cute." Jessie said.

Everyone complimented my pussy. Then we all complimented each other's pussy.

"I love your vaginas." Alice said. "You should always remember that you have to care for and love your vagina as if it is a garden. You won't accept it when someone says nasty things about the garden in your yard, so why should you allow someone say nasty things about your vagina? The vagina isn't just a place that a baby pops out of, it is a beautiful garden. Each one of you should take a sex toy; choose which ever one you want."

There were varieties of sex toys in the room. I chose a bullet vibrator; it was a bronze, lipstick-sized vibrator.

"The sex toys you have chosen, I want you to use it tonight." Alice said, "When you use it, remember how precious your vagina is. The problem with the world is that society kicks against what others have invented for our pleasures but they don't provide an alternate solution." She moved around the room as she talked, "The society frowns against women's masturbation and sex toys. Yet, they have provided no solution on how a woman can take care of herself when she is horny. What should women do when their man is busy sowing his wild oats and doesn't have her time? What should women do when they have a husband who isn't patient enough to give them an orgasm?

What about the lonely married and single women in the world?" She reached for a bottle of water which was on a table and took a mouthful.

We all listened to her with rapt attention. She looked so passionate when she continued to talk.

"The invention of sex toys and dolls is one of the greatest things to ever happen to mankind." Alice went on, "Men and women fantasize about so many things, now with sex toys and dolls they wouldn't be hurting anyone if they indulged in their fantasies. It is better for a man to get a sex doll than for him to force his attention on a woman who doesn't want it. If not for sex toys, so many married women would have cheated on their spouses. I love my orgasm; I love my sex toy and I love myself. I'll see you all tomorrow."

We all cheered. When I glanced at my wrist, we had spent seven hours in the class, I was surprised. I didn't want the class to end. We all wore our clothes. Then we hugged each other and said goodbye. I didn't leave with the other women. I helped Alice put away the yoga mats.

"Alice, I love your class." I said.

"Thank you," she said.

"How long have you been a sex educator?" I asked, as I rolled the last mat.

"I have been a sex educator for twenty years." She replied.

"Wow, that's such a long time." I said, "Why did you choose to be a sex educator? I am sorry for being so inquisitive."

She laughed, "Come with me, I'll make a fresh lemonade for us, and we can eat some of those treats you brought."

I followed Alice into the kitchen. She made a refreshing glass of lemonade, and then we sat at the kitchen table and enjoyed some croissants.

"It's going to be a long story." She smiled at me. "I have the time," I said, grinning.

"I met my husband, Brock, when I was twenty." Alice said, "I was a virgin when I met him. My mother always told my sister, Willow and I that our virginity was a prized possession. She said we could marry well if we protected our virginity. She never allowed us to keep our doors locked, because she didn't want us to touch ourselves the way some 'indecent' girls do." She laughed, "That was the exact word my mother used. She wanted us to make a match that would turn our situation around, we were poor. She had me out of wedlock after Willow's dad passed. Actually, she got pregnant for her married boss. She thought he would leave his wife for her and marry her. She had some wild dreams, that woman."

Alice refilled our glasses. I leaned my head on my palms as I listened to her.

"So, we guarded our virginities," Alice said, "Because we wanted to make a good match and have a financial stable life. However, Willow fell in love with a mechanic and eloped with him. They got married. Mother never forgave Willow for shattering her dreams of having a wealthy son-in-law. So, she threatened to throw me out of the house if I also did what Willow did to her. I wanted to please my mother. I wanted to be a good daughter. So, when Mother introduced me to Brock as my suitor, I agreed to marry him. Brock was a wealthy widower. He was twenty years older than me; he was caring, and he doted on me. Mother was pleased with me; I was happy too. We had a big society wedding and had our honeymoon on a luxurious Island."

"It sounds so romantic," I sighed.

She laughed, "I realized my mistake on our wedding night. Brock switched off the light, lifted the hem of my nightgown and thrust his penis into me. He didn't kiss me or touch my body. Willow had told me how loving making was so much fun, especially if you do it with someone you love. Willow told me that she used to have goosebumps on her skin whenever her husband, John, kissed her. She used to see the stars and have multiple orgasms when he made love to her. I wanted to have what Willow and John had. However, I was disappointed."

"Oh," I said.

"Brock orgasmed after a few trusts," She said, "Then he turned around and started to snore. I just lay there in the dark. My body was pulsating, I didn't know what my body wanted, but there was an ache inside me. That was the start of a miserable, unfulfilled sexual life for me. I had money, maids and I could afford to travel around the world. But the only thing which I needed the most was just to have an orgasm. Our sex life became worse as the years rolled by. Then it got to a point that he didn't even want to have sex with me anymore. He always complained that he was tired. I felt lost and I was lonely. I couldn't talk to Willow about my problems because I was too embarrassed. I couldn't touch myself either because society said it was wrong for a woman to touch herself.

When I started complaining and nagging, Brock threatened to divorce me. He said I had unwholesome desires and that I was an immoral woman."

"That must have really been a tough time for you." I said.

"Yes," She nodded, "He talked to my mother about my 'unwholesomeness.'"

"What did she do?" I asked.

"She screamed at me and called me all sort of names. She said I was ungrateful because she had given me the life my sister could only dream of. But I could see that she was wrong, my sister was happy and content with her life." Alice picked up a croissant and broke off the edge which she put into her mouth, "I didn't want to cheat on my husband even though I met another man whom I fell in love with. He asked me to leave Brock for him, but I was a coward. We never had sex; it was an emotional affair. Anyway, he passed away before I had the courage to leave Brock."

"Oh, that's so sad."

"Yes," She replied, "I started wondering if there were other women like me in the world. I wanted to connect with those women. Sadly, the women in my generation were raised to wear a smile on their face even if they are going through hell. There was no one to talk to. There were so many women like me who had problems in their marriage and their relationship. But they were not willing to talk about it. They would rather cry in secret. I formed a group; I started with my maids who were married. I realized that young, old, rich or poor, all women want love from their spouse and some orgasm. Other women joined the group and we continued to grow. I finally had the courage to ask Brock for a divorce. After the divorce, some of the women started to avoid me because they were scared that I might take an interest in their husband. That's crazy."

"Wow, what did you do?" I asked.

"The group broke apart, but I had already decided to become a professional sex educator for both singles and couples. It took me years before I was certified. But it is a journey that has brought self-discovery and lots of confidence. I have helped many couples to have amazing sex lives."

I was inspired by Alice's story. As I listened to her, I already knew that my purpose on earth was to become a sex educator. I would like to educate young girls about sex and their body.

"Thank you for sharing your story with me," I replied, "You have really inspired me."

She smiled at me, "I'm glad my story inspired you."

"I'd like to pay for the subsequent classes," I said.

She waved her hand, "Don't bother. I appreciate all the treats you asked me to keep. It means a lot to me."

I slid off the stool, "Thank you so much. It is a pleasure to meet you."

"It is a pleasure to meet you too," She replied.

She walked me to the door, waving at me until I turned into another street. The bullet vibrator was in my pocket, occasionally, I felt it to ensure that it was still there. The walk back home was pleasurable. It felt like I was walking on clouds. I felt so happy.

After dinner, I went into my room. I took a refreshing shower and got into bed. I was eager to learn more about being a sex educator. But I wanted to pleasure myself first. The vibrations from the tiny toy felt so strong against my palm. I circled a finger around my clit, moaning. My boobs also needed some attention, so I let my right-hand wander to my breasts.

I traced the tip of the toy on my pussy lips. I felt a sweet sensation in the pit of my stomach. My stomach dipped and fluttered. I ran the tip of the vibrator all over my vulva. A burning sensation started inside me, filling my veins with fire. I glided the toy up and down, over my slit, my labia, slowly moving it back to my clit. I moaned out as a sharp jolt of lightening went through me.

I held the tip of the bullet vibrator against my clit. God, it felt so good. My toes curled as I glided the vibrator over the soft plane of my stomach. It pulsated against my navel. My pussy started to drip. I ran my left hand all over my body, caressing my skin. I squeezed my ass, the inside of my thighs, the curves of my hips. I slid a finger into my pussy, moaning as I placed the tip of the toy on my nipples. I brushed the vibrator up and down over my tips until they were hard. I bit my lips, crying softly as I tripped toward an orgasm. I was gradually mastering my body. I knew where to touch to fuel my arousal. I had discovered some erogenous spot on my body. I pressed the toy against my nipples. I arched my back as a ripple of excitement rushed through me. Then, I placed the tip of the toy against my pussy lips. My body was on fire now. I brushed it across my inner thighs, ran it down my legs and pressed the tip against my butthole. My stomach knotted. I reached out my hand, moving it over my ass. I found my gaping, puckered butthole. An incredible wave of pleasure surged inside me when my finger popped into my anus. The feeling was indescribable. I couldn't stop quivering. My legs felt like jelly and my heart was pounding so fast. I fucked my butthole with the toy, working it in and out. I read online that bullet vibrators could easily get lost in one's butt or pussy. So, I was careful not to let it slip too deep into me. I pulled it out of my butthole, running it along my perineum.

My clit twitched. I started to whimper as multiple waves of orgasm hit me. I held the vibrator against my g-spot. I brushed it up and down over my g-spot until my belly started to tighten again. I had another powerful orgasm. I switched off the toy's vibration and licked my juice off it. I was so exhausted that I fell asleep afterward.

Fortunately, the next day was a Saturday, which meant that there was no class to attend. Nana and I made breakfast because Mom were still asleep. Dad said he didn't want so we sat in the kitchen and ate the breakfast we made. Afterward, I grabbed my purse and left the house. By the time I got to Willow's house, all the other students were around. They were all on their mat, naked. I took off my clothes and joined them. We exchanged pleasantries. Alice was still upstairs so we made ourselves comfortable and made small talk until she came downstairs.

"Hi, lovely ladies," Alice said.

"Hi, Alice," We replied.

"We are going to have so much fun today." She started setting the mood; she switched off the light and put lit candles around the room. "Today, I will teach you about two types of orgasms and how you can achieve them."

The door opened and a lovely woman walked in. She was a platinum blonde; she had a smooth, sexy skin. She wore red lipsticks which made her look mysterious. Without saying a word to us, she took off her clothes.

"Hello ladies," she said.

Alice pecked her on the cheeks, "Ladies, this is Suzy; she's an old student who also became a sex educator."

Suzy was friendly and warm. She chatted with us and made us comfortable. I liked her lively personality and her charming smile.

"There are different types of orgasms," Suzy said, "However; we will focus on the main types of orgasm."

Suzy lay on a mat with her legs spread apart. We all watched her with open fascination.

"The first one is how to use your PC muscles and your entire body to achieve orgasm, just like you are doing kegel exercise. The second type of orgasm is the one where you just squeeze and release. This time of orgasm takes a longer time to build up. All you have to do is to squeeze the muscles and release it. Then you squeeze it again and release it. You will keep doing that until you feel your orgasm build up." Suzy said, "While you are petting your clit, don't forget your vagina. You should pleasure your vagina during orgasm."

There was so much electricity in the air; we were all excited and eager to begin. Suzy showed us how to achieve each of the orgasms. She came so hard; it was beautiful to watch. We all took a sex toy; I took a double-headed vibrator. Suzy showed us how to get the second orgasm, she had another powerful orgasm. When it was our turn, none of us was afraid or shy to use the toy.

I put lube on both ends of the toy, and then I trust one end into my pussy and the other end into my butthole. I didn't want to break my hymen, so I didn't trust it directly into my pussy. Within minutes, my orgasm built up. We were all moaning and whimpering. The toy vibrated against my anal walls, sending electrical tingles up my spine. My breath became raspy. I was moaning and panting at the top of my voice. Jessie screamed out when her orgasm exploded. Then Audrey and Meg came at the same time. My abdomen tightened as the surge of pleasure overwhelmed me. I bucked my waist, thrusting the dildo harder into my butthole. I groaned as my orgasm shattered. Meg and Emily sobbed when they had an orgasm for the first time in years. It was a beautiful moment for all of us.

"You all went home with a toy yesterday, tell us about the adventure you had with your toy." Alice said.

We all took turns to narrate how we used our toys. She seemed very pleased; she had a smile on her face the entire time.

"There have been so many misconceptions around the female masturbation." Alice said, "Female masturbation is more than lying on your back and rubbing your vagina until you climax. I have heard some crazy things about masturbation that made me laugh so hard until tears ran down my cheeks," Alice said, laughing, "Masturbation won't make you rich or poor. But it will definitely make you feel good. The only thing is that you should have a control over it; don't let it become the center of your life. Masturbation won't make you go to hell or become infertile."

I lifted my hand, "All my life, I've been told to keep myself for my husband. I have been told that I shouldn't have sex unless I am legally married. Will a man still want to marry me if he knows that I masturbate?"

"If he is a religious fanatic, he won't marry you." Alice said, "But do you know what? Darling, you don't need such a man in your life. It's your body and you own it."

The other women clapped.

"Masturbation has some health benefits that no woman should miss out on," Alice said, "Masturbation will also enhance your sex life. It is pleasurable but it can't replace sex because they are two different things. Rebecca, when you have sex, you'll realize that it is an enjoyable pleasure too but it's not like masturbation. With sex, you'll be able to hold your partner, feel their skin against your palms. You can cuddle after sex or lay in each other's arms. Sex is a great thing. Masturbation is also a great thing. However, you may not always have an orgasm during sex or even enjoy it. Masturbation can give you all the pleasures your partner couldn't give you. Thank you all. This is the end of the class. I'll have another workshop next week for couples, if you are interested, you can sign up on my website."

"Thank you, Alice," We cried.

"I'm going to give you all an assignment," She said, "I want you to discover all the types of orgasms. You should try to give yourself an orgasm, maybe six, seven, eight, nine or even ten. You will give yourself those orgasms in one night. It will help you know your body better. However, you are only allowed to focus on one body part at a time."

Suzy poured everyone a glass of wine. I had never drunk wine before; it was the most amazing thing I ever tasted. It had a little sour taste, and it had some alcohol in it.

Chapter VIII

Twelve Orgasms

I didn't do the assignment right away. I waited a few days to do it because I wanted to prepare my body for it. I carried out some research and I found out that one could orgasm by stimulating or massaging other body parts like the foot, ankle, calf, nipples etc. So, I decided to give myself twelve orgasms in one night. Most people just dive into masturbation by rubbing their clits until they come. I wanted to see if other parts of my body could give me an intense orgasm. Fortunately, there are toys for every erogenous spot on our body. I surfed my favorite toy website, putting everything that caught my fancy into the shopping basket. I bought a silicone nipple massager, clitoris sucking vibrator, a pair of cuffs, silky, pink-colored blindfold, butt plugs, lubes, and a dual motor vibrator. My shopping cart was filled with over ten sex toys, and I was still ready to explore with more.

The toys arrived the following evening when we were about to go to the evening service in church. I asked my family to go ahead, that I would join them. I took the toys into my room, locked the door and went to join. I loved the evening service because the pastor wouldn't preach for a long time. The evening service was usually a time to study the Bible and sing praises to God. This evening, the drummer wasn't around so someone else played the drums.

After the church service, Nana and Mom went to greet the pastor's wife.

Pastor Paul wanted to have a meeting with the men, so Dad stayed behind. I walked out of the church, and I saw the youths. They were whispering about something. I walked over to them, curious to know what they were arguing about.

"Hi guys," I called. "What's going on?"

A redheaded girl named Adele, turned to me, "Haven't you heard?"

"Heard what?"

"Brother Stanley, the drummer has been arrested." Adele said.

"What did he do?" I asked.

"He was selling coke," She replied, "But that's not all."

"Oh my god," I cried, "He's selling hard drugs?"

"He is also a sex offender." She said, "He tried to rape his brother's wife."

I couldn't believe my ears. Brother Stanley seemed like a saint. He doesn't speak much but he always had a kind word to say to everyone. Adele and I walked away from the group. She was eighteen years old, tall and skinny. There were splatters of freckles on her face.

"How do you know all these?" I asked.

"It's all over the news," She sighed.

"Has anybody gone to see him?" I asked.

"No," She replied.

"His family and everyone have abandoned him." Adele said.

"But shouldn't they try to see him?" I asked.

"The church has hurt so many people." She said, "There are some wolves in the church who acts like a sheep. Brother Stanley is one of those wolves." Then she looked behind her, trying to see if there was anyone behind us.

"No one can hear us," I said.

We had walked far away from the church and there wasn't anyone behind us.

"Do you know what happened to the pastor's daughter?"

"Which of the pastor's daughters are you talking about?" I asked.

"The blonde girl, Annalisa," Adele said, "She got pregnant. Her family didn't want anyone to know about it. So, they sent her oversea. When she has the baby, she will return to the church and her parents will legally adopt the child. They plan to make up some wild story about the baby."

I gasped, "Shut up, that's not true!"

"Well, it's the truth." Adele said. "Everyone in the church has a secret. So don't let anyone fool you."

"Why did the pastor conceal his daughter's pregnancy?" I asked, "Last year when Janet, the usher, got pregnant out of wedlock, she was punished. She couldn't work in the church anymore because she had brought shame upon it. I think everyone made life miserable for her because she and her family moved away."

"There is so much hypocrisy in the church," Adele replied, "People pretend as if they are saints so the world can praise them. Everyone has a skeleton in their cupboard."

I had always thought Adele was a shy, quiet girl. I had no idea that she could be so observant and outspoken.

"Yeah, you are right." I replied, "The best thing is to have a good heart and obey the Lord's commandment."

"Yeah," She replied. "Most times we forget that pastors and spiritual leaders are humans. They make mistakes too and they can also be tempted by the devil. Some people worship their pastor instead of God. My mom, Oh Lord, she drives me crazy! She thinks the sun rises and sets on Pastor Paul and his wife! She doesn't know she is neglecting her family. She has lost her mind; she can't make any decision without consulting the pastor and his wife. She claims that she needs their spiritual guidance."

I sighed, "How long has this been going on?"

She pulled in a deep breath, "You know, everyone thinks my dad is dead because of my mom. She is a divorcee."

"Wait a minute! You mean your dad is still alive?" I asked. "Whenever they are praying for widows, your mom is always among them."

"She's crazy." Adele said, "she said my dad is dead to her. She doesn't want anyone to know she is divorced. My brother and I are tired of her. We plan to move away as soon as we are done with college."

"I am sorry." I said, "My parents are having problems too; I wish they can seek professional help. But Mom is too stubborn. She says Jesus will handle it."

"Jesus didn't say we shouldn't seek for help when we need it." Adele said.

Soon, Adele's house came into view.

"Thank you, Adele, you can call me if you ever need someone to talk to," I said.

She sighed, "Thank you. I'll see you tomorrow."

"Yeah, goodnight,"

We all had a spare key to our house, so I let myself into the house. I brought out my new sex toys from the toy box. I was giddy with excitement. My skin felt cool after I took a shower. I wanted to give myself twelve orgasms; I was thrilled by the idea of climaxing twelve times.

I started with my breasts, gently rubbing my hands around them. I wanted to orgasm just by stimulating my nipples. I circled my fingers around my areolas. A sizzling sensation ran through me. My fingers moved across my nipples, back and forth. Other parts of my body began to throb, but I focused on my nipples alone. My nipples were so sensitive. I almost climaxed when I placed the nipple sucker on my nipples. It felt like someone was sucking my nipples. I started to massage my boobs, moaning softly. After a while I pulled off the nipple sucker, my nipples were hard to the touch. They were so engorged and tender. My stomach began to flutter, out of excitement. Fireworks exploded inside me. My heart started hammering against my chest. Waves after waves of pleasure washed over me. I placed the nipple sucker on my right nipple while rolling my left nipple between my fingers. Sensations coiled around my body. I saw myself floating on a fluffy, colorful sky.

I was in paradise. The hot, intense sensations spread over my body. My skin started to tingle. My pussy was dripping juice.

I moistened my fingers with my saliva; then I rubbed it over my nipples. My abdomen clenched as a surge of pleasure raced through me. I pulled off the nipple sucker on my right nipple, giving both nipples a squeeze. I put some pressure on my breasts. My nipples throbbed harder. I pinched my nipples, and a bolt of lightning went through me. Saliva dribbled out of my mouth. My lips wouldn't stop quivering. My entire body shook. I squeezed my breasts, so hard, that a tingly pain shot through me. Waves of pleasure filled my body. I cried out when my orgasm shattered. My entire body convulsed until the moment passed. My cheeks were wet with my tears. I ran my hand over my pussy, my precious garden. I rubbed a finger between the moist folds of my pussy. I brushed the pad of my fingers against my clit, up and down. My juice rushed out of me, spreading over my inner thighs.

Then I pinched my clit.

"Hmmmn,"

I could feel the pleasure as it builds inside me. I stroked my labia, running a finger up and down. My waist jerked, involuntarily, slamming against my hand. My toes began to curl up as sensations swept over me. My pussy walls trembled, throbbing so hard. I wanted to slam a finger into myself and fill up the ache inside me with pleasure. My fingers slide over my clit again and my orgasm exploded.

I licked my lips, groaning softly. I heard footsteps outside my door, it was Mom. My door was locked but I didn't want to see anyone. I breathed with relief when she walked away. I crawled to the foot of the bed; I lay on my stomach, brushing my fingers across my clit. My spine stiffened. I couldn't feel my legs anymore. My wrist ached a little but there was a volcano inside me. I bit my lips when a powerful orgasm rippled through me.

"Two down," I said, "I owe my body ten more orgasms,"

I didn't know where to focus on next, so I took the new blindfold that I bought. I slid the blindfold over my eyes as I reached for a vibrator. I let my hand wander over my body.

I wanted to randomly pick a body part. When my fingers touched my foot, an electrical shock buzzed through me. I reached out my hand, searching for a bottle of massage oil. I poured the oil over my feet and my ankles. I didn't know if I could achieve orgasm if I massaged my feet, but I wanted to try it. I started to massage my feet, pulling and tugging on my toes. Each little tug sent a tingle up my spine. I rubbed the short length of my toes with my fingers. Then I massaged the sole of my feet. My fingers accidentally brushed against a spot on my ankles. Lord, it felt so good. I squeezed my calves, moaning. My toes were giving me so much pleasure; something I never imagined could be possible. My body was flexible, so I tilted my head forward while pressing my legs against my chest. I took my toes into my mouth; it was the most amazing thing that I had discovered. The sensation, the sweet, amazing feelings brought tears to my eyes. I ran my fingers along the back of my legs, putting pressure on the muscles around my calves. I dug my fingers into a spot above my ankles; gosh, it was amazing. I kissed and suckled my toes as I massaged and stimulated my feet. I found a muscle behind my legs that fuelled my arousal. My toes curled, hard, as I climaxed. I continued to squeeze, caress and massage my legs. When my fingers touched the spot between my ankles and my Achilles tendon; another wave of orgasm shot through me.

I started to wonder if I could climax by massaging my neck. I started to breathe gently. My chest rose and fell as my breath became raspy. My sexual pleasure heightened as I started to massage my shoulders. I lifted the blindfold off my face so I could see. I picked up a massage wand which also doubled as a vibrator. I ran the wand across my shoulders. The vibrating massage wand pulsated against my shoulder blades. It felt like a gentle tap against my skin. I oiled my fingers, wrapping them around my neck. I stroked the back of my neck, brushing my fingers against my skin. When I sank my fingers into my shoulders, I felt a frisson of excitement. I started moving my fingers down my back, putting pressure on my skin with the heels of my palms. I pounded my back with my fists. Then I rubbed the sides of my back, spreading my skin with my fingers.My pussy throbbed as my juice shot out of me. I squeezed my right shoulder, sliding my fingers over it until they touched my collarbone. I felt the muscles around my shoulders contract. I started to put pressure on my neck, rolling the skin between my fingers. Finally, I found a muscle knot in my right shoulder. I started to elongate my muscles with my fingers, relaxing the nerves around my neck. The muscle started to soften between my fingers. My pussy was dripping so much. I didn't want the sexual tension, thrill and pleasure to end. I wanted to delay my sexual release for as long as possible. I had hot and cold, feverish sensations. I stretched, fondled and massaged my shoulders until the flesh around there felt like jelly. I started to moan when a fluttery sensation filled my stomach. My clit twitched, jerking back and forth. When the orgasm hit me, I cried out. My body trembled until the effect of the orgasm subsided. I was astonished. I wanted to scream it out, to the world that I just came by rubbing my neck.

The next orgasm that I wanted to give myself was a G-spot orgasm. Just like the clit, some women don't give their G-spot the attention it needs. I fondled my vulva, squeezing my pussy lips. I squeezed the muscles around the opening of my pussy. God, that was so amazing. I used my index finger and my forefinger to squeeze my outer lips. Then I reached for my clit and rubbed my thumb over it. A moan tumbled out of my mouth as I arched my back in ecstasy. I licked my forefinger, sucking on it as if it was a dick. I almost climaxed again. My body was already so sensitive, craving for another toe-curling, nerve-tingling and back- arching orgasm. If my body could speak, it would scream out of frustration. I knew what my body wanted, but I didn't want to rush it. I wanted to take things slow and enjoy every moment. I pushed a finger into my pussy. My pussy walls felt warm and tight around my finger. My butthole expanded a little as it began to tingle. I wanted to finger both my butthole and my pussy at the same time, but the instruction was to focus on one body part at a time. I curled my finger inside me, sighing as a tingle spread across my body.

My nipples were aching, and my belly was taut with need. I didn't penetrate myself deeply because I still wanted my hymen to be intact. I ground my waist against my hand, tugging on my nipples with my other hand. I felt a jolt of lightening when my finger brushed against my G-spot. The soft, spongy tissue on the upper wall of my pussy started to swell against my finger. I could feel my G-spot swell; it was an incredible sensation. I started to feel an ache in my bladder, the tingly sweetness spread across my body like wildfire. It felt like I wanted to pee, but I knew it wasn't urine that was trying to come out of me; it was feminine squirt. I started to rub my clit as I stimulated my G-spot with my finger. My hips and pelvis began to move, following the twirling movement of my finger. I could have sworn the orgasm I had was the best, the greatest, the sweetest. My whole body shook for what seemed like an eternity to me.

I tried to stop trembling, but I couldn't.

I was already breathless, and beads of perspiration had formed on my forehead. My windows were locked, if not my family would have heard my screams of ecstasy. At that point, I realized I wouldn't be able to give myself twelve orgasms in one night. My heart hammered against my chest. My legs felt like jelly; my pussy walls were throbbing as they dripped. The muscles in my body were jerking, pulsating. I started to squirt again even though I had stopped touching myself.

When my breathing calmed, I rubbed a finger around my butthole. It seemed like my butthole was filled with electrical charged nerves. As I orbited my finger around my butthole, deep pulsating waves of pleasure radiated through my body. My butt plug was ready to be used; ready to fill up my anal cavity. My butthole was leaking. I put some lubricant on the tip of the butt plug. My anus was already lubricated by my juice, but I still put some lube around it. I wanted to make this magical, lusty anal voyage enjoyable. The entire nerves in my butthole started to tingle; I curved two fingers and shoved them into my anus. My rectum tightened around my fingers, making me feel as if I wanted to defecate. I moaned out as I pressed the tip of the butt plug against my nether hole.

Taking deep breaths, I eased the butt plug into my anus. Electricity sparked off inside me, the sparks made me spasm. I started to put pressure on my butthole, moving the toy in and out. The plug vibrated as it glided into me, stretching my anal walls. I started to squirt again. I covered my mouth with my hands so I wouldn't wake the entire neighborhood. My bedsheet was damp with my juice and sweat. The pulsations in my anus became too much for me to handle. Tears rushed down my cheeks as my body convulsed over and over. I pulled the butt plug out of my anus, sliding two fingers into my anal cavity. I stroked and stimulated my anal walls with my fingers. My clit jerked as another wave of pleasure washed over me. I pulled my wet fingers out of my asshole. I began to massage my tiny, puckered hole. I slid the tip of my finger in and out of my rectum. I loved the way my anal ring squeezed my finger as if it was trying to hug it. I penetrated my asshole with my forefinger as I orbited my index finger around the puckered, dusky rim.

My knees jerked. I curled the finger that was inside my anus as if I was indicating to someone to come forward. My finger grazed the tissues around my anal walls. I felt a slight pressure on my rectum. My orgasm rapidly built up, overwhelming me. I squeezed my butt cheeks as I started to slide my finger out of my anus. I had another explosive orgasm. I shoved my face into my pillow, moaning. The radiation increased.

Pleasure waves sailed through me. My body was covered with sweat.

I couldn't give myself twelve orgasms because I was exhausted and sated. My body continued to shake for hours.

Could anyone really give themselves twelve orgasms in one night? One day, I may be able to give myself twelve orgasms in one night.

Chapter IX

My First Kiss

"You look so tense," Adele said, laughing. "Haven't you been to a party before?"

"The last time I went to a party was when I was seven," I said. "My mother and grandmother took me to the party. They didn't allow me to participate in any of the fun activities because they weren't things that Christians do."

"Don't worry, I won't tell anyone." She said, still laughing.

Adele's friend, Eva, had a big brother who was in college. Their parents weren't in town, so Eva's brother was throwing a party for his friends. I had never met either Eva or her brother, but I couldn't say no when Adele invited me to the party. It was a Friday night; my family had a vigil in church, but I told them I wasn't feeling well. So, they allowed me to stay at home. Eva's house was only a few streets away.

"So, you've never had a boyfriend?" Adele asked.

"Do you have a boyfriend?" I asked.

She grinned, "I have a boyfriend. I'll introduce you to him soon."

I grinned at her. It was so easy to love her. She was cheerful, easy-going and full of life.

She started talking about her boyfriend, describing her first kiss and the way she felt.

They had been dating for a year. I was fascinated.

"Your first kiss sound like something that would happen in fairytales," I said, licking my lips.

She suddenly stopped talking and grabbed my hand. Her face contorted with pain.

"Are you alright," I asked.

She rolled her eyes, "Becky, you've never kissed too?"

We both burst into laughter.

"It's not my fault," I said. "How do I get my first kiss when I haven't had a boyfriend?"

"You mean no boy asked you to date him or tried to kiss you?" She asked.

"A few boys asked me to be their girlfriend," I replied, scrunching up my nose, "They were wild boys, my family wouldn't approve."

"Oh, Becky," She replied.

I wrapped my hands around my body as we approached the house. I could hear the loud sound of music. There were several cars parked in front of the house. She opened a little gate and we walked in. A young, dark-haired girl in jeans and a white shirt walked out of the house. Her face lit up when she saw us. She rushed towards us and embraced Adele.

"Hi Eva," Adele cried.

"Hey, I am glad you came, the party is so boring," Eva said.

"Oh, really?" Adele asked, "Meet my friend, Becky."

"Hi," I said.

Eva embraced me, "It's nice to meet you, Becky."

"It's a pleasure to meet you." I replied.

"Come in," she said.

We walked into the house which was filled with college boys and girls. I understood why the party seemed boring to Eva because most of the people at the party were older than her. Adele and Eva went upstairs while I remained in the living room. A boy passed me a red party cup while another boy poured a drink into the cup for me. Some of them were dancing while others sat on the couch, smoking from a bong and drinking. A few minutes later, Adele came down the stairs.

"Do you want to come upstairs? We can eat pizza and watch a movie on Eva's laptop," Adele said, "Eva is right, this party is boring. Her brother didn't let her invite anyone from my school."

"I think I will stay downstairs for a while." I said, "I'll come up when I am bored."

"Okay." Adele said.

I returned to the party, walking through the crowd. I saw another door which led into the yard. I went into the yard and stood there for a while. As I made to go back into the house, I bumped into someone. I looked up and stared into the sexiest eyes I had ever seen. He didn't look offended. Instead, he looked amused. He was tall and handsome. I loved the curly locks of hair on his head.

"I'm so sorry." I said.

"Hey, it's fine," he said.

I loved the sound of his voice. My stomach dipped as butterflies swam around in it.

"I think I have seen you somewhere…" He said as a serious look appeared on his face.

His face didn't seem familiar, so I was certain he was trying to use a pickup line on me. I whirled around and headed towards the living room.

"Rebecca," He called.

I paused.

"I saw you at the orphanage." He said.

I turned around to face him. He shortened the distance between us, and I caught a whiff of his musky cologne.

My heart raced with excitement.

"Do you also volunteer at the orphanage?" I asked.

"Yes," He replied. "I am Luke Anderson."

"Umm," I swallowed hard, "Rebecca Hayes,"

"Do you want to go in?" He asked, "Sorry, I've been such a terrible host. What do I offer you?"

"Are you Eva's brother?" I asked.

"Yeah," He grinned, "Do you know my sister?"

"I met her tonight," I replied, "Eva's friend, Adele, invited me to the party. I hope you don't mind."

"Wait, you are in High school?" He asked.

"No," I laughed, "I'm in my second year in the community college."

"Oh, I'm sorry." He said, "I'm also in my second year but I don't school around here, Illinois State University. I wanted to be far away from my family."

We walked into the garden and sat on the grass.

"What are you majoring in?" I asked.

"It's Mathematics," he said.

"Math?" I was surprised.

He laughed, sending warm waves of pleasure through me.

"I know I don't look like a nerd." Luke said, "How about you, what are you studying?"

"Occupational Therapy," I replied.

"That's a good course," he said. "Is that why you volunteer at the orphanage?"

"Well, my family chose that course for me." I replied, "I volunteer at the orphanage because I love the children. Recently, I discovered a new passion and I'd like to pursue a career in it."

"Really?" He asked. "What is it?"

"Sex," I said, blushing.

He didn't laugh.

"You'd like to be a sex therapist?"

"Yeah, something like that," I replied.

"It's a great career." He said, "Sex Therapists are highly sought-after professionals. Apart from the fact that they make lots of money, they also help couples with their sexual problems."

"You really think it's a great idea?" I asked.

"Of course," He replied, "You can obtain a master's degree in therapy or psychology. You can also get some professional degrees; it will make it easier for you to get a job.

Most therapists have their own business, but you can work for others for a few years to gain some experience in the field."

"Thank you, Luke," I replied, "Thanks for the encouragement. I don't think my family will approve but this is what I want."

"Don't let anyone stop you from achieving your dreams," Luke replied, "Do you know why? You'll regret it for the rest of your life."

"Yeah, that's true." I replied, tucking a strand of hair behind my ear. We looked at each other for a few minutes. I felt the chemistry between us.

"Do you want to drink anything?" He asked.

"No, thanks." I replied. "Why do you volunteer at the orphanage?"

"I was adopted." He replied, "I was found on the doorsteps of the orphanage, and I lived there until I was ten."

"Oh," I said, "Do you hate talking about it?"

"No," He replied, "It's like I am giving back to the people who gave me a home for ten years. I only volunteer whenever I am at home."

"That's nice." I replied.

"The children love you." He said, "they told me about you and the things you and your grandmother do for them. They said you are an angel."

I laughed, "I'm sure they were exaggerating."

"I don't think they exaggerated," He replied, "You are an angel."

My heart skipped. My gaze drifted to his again, I couldn't hold back myself anymore. I leaned close to him and placed a soft kiss on his lips. Then I pulled backward and stood up.

"Goodbye, Luke," I said.

"Wait," he said.

He pulled me into his arms, placing his arms around me. Then he tilted my head backward and his mouth covered mine. His warm tongue slipped into my mouth, teasing me until I moaned out. His tongue swept across the roof of my mouth. He kissed me, passionately. I tried to kiss him back, but I didn't get it right. So, he taught me how to kiss him. He was so gentle and patient with me. One of his hands was on my lower back; he pressed a soft kiss to the corners of my mouth. Then he traced the contours of my lips with his. I moaned, softly. He kissed me hard and our tongues danced for several minutes. I felt goosebumps on my skin as pleasure surged inside me.

He broke off the kiss and I placed my head on his chest. I felt his strong heartbeat. I didn't want to go home; I wanted to be in Luke's arms forever.

"I like you," He whispered to me.

There was a possibility that he was lying but I believed him. I liked him too.

"Me too,"

"I'd like to see you again." He said.

I wanted to see him again too.

"When are you going back to school?" I asked.

"We are on break," He replied.

"Umm, okay, I guess I'll see you at the orphanage."

"Okay. I'll walk you back home."

"I have to tell Adele I am leaving." I replied.

"Wait here, I'll go get her." He said.

He went into the house and walked out with Adele.

"I need to go back home." I said.

Adele frowned, "I thought you'd stay until morning."

"No, I can't." I replied.

"I'll go get my jacket so we can leave." Adele replied.

"No, you don't have to go back with me if you don't want to." I replied.

She turned to Luke, "Please can you walk her home?"

"It would be my pleasure." Luke said.

"Thanks, Luke," Adele said.

Adele hugged me before she went back into the house.

"Do you want me to drive, or you'd rather walk?" He asked.

"Let's walk," I said, "My house is only a few blocks away."

"Alright." He replied.

As we walked down the street, he held my hand and it felt so right. He wasn't a church boy, but he seemed sweet and caring.

"Can I take you to dinner tomorrow?" He asked.

"Okay," I replied.

His lips curved into a smile. "Where do you want us to go?"

"You can choose the place," I replied.

"Okay," He said, "Do you mind if I pick you up from your home and what time should I pick you up?"

"You can pick me up by 5 pm," I replied.

His smile widened. He seemed genuinely happy.

It would be my first date; I was a little nervous and excited at the same time. When we got to my house, he walked me up to the porch.

"I'm really glad I met you tonight, Rebecca," he said.

"Me too," I replied. "Thanks for walking me home."

"It is my pleasure," He replied.

I opened the door and walked into the house.

"Goodnight, Luke," I said.

"Goodnight, Rebecca." He lifted his hand, waving at me.

I closed the door, but I didn't go into my room. I peered through the window, watching him until I couldn't see him anymore. I felt my lips with my hand; I just had my first kiss. I would never forget that wonderful moment.

Chapter X

First Date

"You are going on a date?" Mom asked. "Is he someone we know? Is he a Christian?"

"Is he a church member?" Nana asked.

Mom and Nana didn't give me a chance to answer their question. Instead, they kept asking one question after another until I got frustrated. I walked out of the living room and went back into my room. Some minutes later, Mom knocked on my door. She sat beside me on the bed; she looked so tired and unhappy.

"I'm sorry." She said.

"It's okay, Mom," I replied, "I know you are looking out for me."

She bowed her head, "I don't deserve you. Rebecca, you are the best thing to ever happen to me."

Mom had never said anything like this to me before.

"Awww, Mom," I said.

"I wanted to talk to you about something," She said, "I thought if I ignore it, all the problems will go away."

"What's wrong Mom?" I asked.

"It's about your dad," She replied.

That was when I realized I hadn't seen Dad. He didn't return home after the prayer vigil.

"Did something happen to him?" I asked.

"No," She replied. "He moved out."

"What?" I cried, "Why?"

"The devil has gotten into him." She replied.

"What happened?" I asked.

"He wants a divorce," She replied, "He's been having an affair with another woman. Even when he was here, his heart was never here."

"Mom," I cried, "How could he do this? I am so sorry."

"We'll be fine."

"What are you going to do?" I asked.

She looked so lost, "I don't know."

"Do you want this divorce?" I asked, "What are we going to do? You can't just give up on your marriage."

"What do you want me to do?" She cried, "I have prayed so hard. I have done everything a good wife should do."

"Mom," I said.

She wiped away the tears on her cheeks, "What time is that boy picking you up?"

"5 pm," I replied, "When did Dad move out?"

"He told me this morning that he wants to move out and he also asked me for a divorce." Mom replied.

"Dear Lord," I said, "How could Dad do this to us?"

"I don't want to live my life like Mrs. Shaw who pretends to be a widow." Mom said.

I gasped, "You knew Adele's mom wasn't a widow?"

Mom smiled, "Everyone knows her husband is alive. She thinks we are stupid, but the joke is on her."

Mom and I laughed. I embraced her and she held me.

"I am so sorry, Mom." I said, "I'll talk to Dad, if you can forgive him…"

She stepped backward, "I don't think I can ever forgive him. He really hurt me."

"I'm sorry Mom."

"What's your boyfriend's name?"

"He's not my boyfriend." I replied, "He only asked me to have dinner with him."

She folded her arms across her chest, "What is his name?"

"Luke," I replied, "He also volunteers at the orphanage."

She nodded her head, "I know him but he's not a Christian,"

"Mom!" I said.

She headed towards the door and then she turned around, "It is your duty to make him accept Christ. If he doesn't accept Christ, I'm sorry; I won't give you, my blessing."

I sighed as she walked out of the room. I was looking forward to the date but at that moment, I just wanted to crawl under my duvet and sleep. I didn't understand why Dad would have an affair or want to leave Mom. If they had problems, why couldn't they talk to a counselor? He was trying to break our family apart for selfish reasons. I thought Dad was a godly man, but it seemed like I didn't know his true colors. Tears stung my eyes; I blinked until the moment passed.

I didn't know what to wear for my first date, after much deliberation, I decided to wear jeans with a top and jacket. Nana came into my room; she held my hands and prayed for me. Then she hugged me.

By 5 pm, Luke knocked on the door. He brought a bottle of sweet wine and flowers for both mom and Nana. He managed to charm both women and promised to bring me home before midnight. I tried not to think of Dad as he opened the passenger door of his car. He acted like a gentleman all through the dinner. Afterward, he drove to the river and parked his car.

"Are you okay?" He asked.

"You've been so quiet tonight."

"I am sorry," I said.

"Please, don't apologize," He replied, "Do you want to talk about it?"

"My dad moved out of the house," I said, "I wasn't close to him, but I feel betrayed. He always told me family comes first, yet, he is trying to break our family apart."

"I'm sorry," He said, squeezing my hand, "Have you reached out to him? You should talk to him you might not be able to change his mind but talking to him might make you feel better. Are they willing to see a counselor?"

"No," I replied. "He had an affair, he betrayed her."

He placed an arm around me, hugging me. It felt good to have someone to talk to; a shoulder to lean on. I planted a kiss on his lips as I placed my fingers on the sides of his face. He allowed me to kiss him and explore his mouth. When I started unbuttoning his shirt, he held my hand.

"Rebecca, you are vulnerable at this moment," He whispered, "I don't think this is a good idea."

I wrapped my hands around him, hugging him. He was right, I wasn't thinking right, and I might regret any actions I took now.

"I have a better idea," Luke said, "Let's cuddle,"

"Umm, that's a good idea." I replied.

He held me in his arms, pressing his warm body against mine.

"Have you ever had a girlfriend?" I asked.

"Yes," He replied, "My ex-girlfriend and I broke up two months ago,"

"Why?" I asked.

He sighed, "It was my fault, I was too busy; I didn't have time for her. I wasn't there for her when she needed me. It's a crazy story."

"I want to hear it; if you don't mind."

He sighed, "My girlfriend and I were supposed to hang out. I had been too busy with my studies, but I promised to take her to dinner the weekend we broke up. Earlier that day she lost her dog, she had the dog since she was a child. It meant a lot to her because she didn't have any siblings."

"Oh, that's so sad." I said.

"Yes," He replied, "She called me that she was coming over and I asked her to come. But I forgot about it because I was in the library, caught up in the world of calculations. So, she went to my room and met my roommate. Anyway, they fell for each other. They are still together."

"Oh, wow." I said, "Were you hurt?"

"I deserved it." He replied. "I guess they were destined to be together."

"I'd have been hurt." I said, "Are you still friends with them?"

"No, I kicked my roommate out." He replied.

"Are you always this honest?" I asked.

"I always try my best to say the truth." He replied.

I giggled, "What's the craziest thing you've ever done?"

He laughed, "Are you sure you want me to talk about that?"

"Yeah," I replied.

"I bought sex toys for my ex-girlfriend when we were on school break," He replied, "I bought it online and asked the company to deliver it to her. However, she and her mom have the same first name."

"Oh Lord," I said, laughing.

"So, they delivered the sex toys to Mrs. Violet Williams, instead of Miss Violet Williams," he said.

We both started laughing so hard. He brushed his fingers across my lips.

"I love the sound of your laughter." He said.

He gazed into my eyes for a few minutes. Then he leaned over and kissed me. The kiss made me feel warm all over. His tongue stroked the inside of my mouth. Luke stroked my hair as he kissed me, heatedly. Warmth filled my body; I didn't want the kiss to end. I straddled his thighs, opening the first button on his shirt. I planted a soft kiss on his throat.

He groaned. I opened another button and touched his bare skin.

"I love to use sex toys," I said.

"Hmmmn, that's so sexy," He replied. "Are you trying to turn me on?"

I giggled. He stroked the sides of my arms as he started to kiss me again. After a while, he lifted my waist and set me on the grass.

"What are you doing on Monday?" He asked.

"I don't know yet." I replied.

"I'd like to take you to the movies," He said, "Or is there anywhere you want to go?"

"Movies," I said.

He grinned at me.

We continued to talk until the weather became cold. He wrapped his arms around me, sharing his body warmth with me. The moon was up in the sky, so it illuminated the environment.

Then he scratched his hair as a sheepish look crossed his face.

"What is it?" I asked.

"Excuse me." He said.

He opened a compartment and brought out a parcel. Then he returned to me and placed it on my thighs.

"I wanted to give this to you when I came to your house." He said, "But I was so nervous that I forgot. I am sorry."

My lips curled into a smile, "What is it?"

"Open it," he said.

My fingers trembled as I removed the ribbon on the box. He got me a box of white chocolate which had different shapes. No one boy had ever given me a gift. My heart fluttered; I felt butterflies swimming around in my stomach.

"Thank you." I said.

"You are welcome." He said, looking at the time, "I promised your family I would bring you back home on time."

I sighed, "Yeah,"

"I wish this day wouldn't come to an end," he said.

"Me too," I replied.

Chapter XI

The Big Fight

Luke dropped me off at home and he walked me to the porch. We didn't know if my family was watching through the window, so we didn't kiss. He held my hand, squeezing it. Then he whispered into my ears.

"Thanks, I had a great time."

"Me too," I replied.

"About your dad…" He said, "Will you contact him?"

"Yes, I will," I replied.

"If you need anything or you feel like talking to someone…" He touched his shoulders, "They are wide enough to lean on."

I giggled, "I'll remember that whenever I need a shoulder to lean on."

He pecked me on the cheek, "Goodnight, I'll call you when I get home."

"Goodnight, Luke," I said, "Once again, thanks for the gift."

"You are welcome,"

I walked into the house and closed the door. I watched through the window and stood there until Luke drove away.

Then I walked into my room, I was surprised to see Mom sitting on my bed. She had her face between her palms. It seemed like she was crying. I placed the box of chocolate on the bed. As I moved closer to her, I noticed the overnight bag beside her.

"Mom, are you going somewhere?" I asked, "What are you doing in my room?"

She didn't reply, she continued to sob. I knelt beside her, placing a hand on her thighs.

"Mom, you are scaring me," I said, "Please talk to me."

She didn't respond. She continued to cry so hard, the sound broke my heart. When I couldn't get her to talk to me, I went to get my grandmother.

"What happened?" Nana asked.

Still, Mom didn't say anything. Nana and I were worried about her. Then she stood and faced me.

"I found the stuff under your bed," she said.

"What?" Nana asked.

I didn't feel ashamed, instead, I was annoyed.

"I kept it there because I didn't want you to see it," I replied, "How did you see it?"

"Why would you have such things in your room?" She asked.

"What is going on here?" Nana asked.

"You shouldn't have gone through my things," I replied, "I am an adult, I am not a teenager anymore."

"Becky, don't talk to your mother like that." Nana cautioned.

"You are living under my roof," Mom said, "I don't care what you say you are; I won't let you invite the devil into this house."

"Maybe the devil is already in this house," I retorted.

"Keep quiet, child," Nana said, "What is this? Why are you two bickering at each other? Rebecca, have you forgotten the Lord's commandment? What has gotten into you?"

"Nana, I don't want her going through my stuff," I replied, "I need my privacy."

"What did you find in her room?" Nana asked Mom.

Mom pulled out the large sex toy box under my bed. She placed it on the bed, pouring the contents on the bed, making them fly in every direction. I got pissed and started picking up my precious sex toys.

"What is wrong with you, Mom?" I asked, "What is wrong in using a sex toy?"

"So, you are no longer a virgin?" She asked. "I am still a virgin," I replied, "But with or without my virginity, I am still human and losing my virginity wouldn't diminish my worth in the eyes of a man who genuinely loves me." I shoved the toys into the box.

"Come on, let's go, we'll talk about this tomorrow." Nana said to Mom.

"No, mother," She replied, "We need to talk about this now. You can't stay under this roof anymore. I won't live under the same roof with someone who has these demonic objects in her room."

"Don't be a hypocrite; Mom," I said. "Sex toys have lots of benefits; don't tell me you haven't used them before."

"Do you know what?" She asked, "You need to leave this house, you can't stay here anymore."

"That's the best news I've heard in a long time," I said, "I see you went through the trouble of packing a bag for me, thanks Mom."

"You can't leave that stuff here," She said, "You have to take them with you."

"My pleasure," I replied.

"So, you are going to leave?" Nana asked me.

I grabbed my bag, holding the box under my arm.

"She asked me to leave," I replied.

"No, child," Nana replied, "You have to stay here, we can talk about this tomorrow,"

"No, I want her to leave right now." Mom cried.

I was so hurt.

"Maybe that's why Dad left you for another woman," I muttered under my breath, but she heard me.

"What did you say?" Mom asked.

"I said maybe that's why Dad left you, because you are frigid."

She stiffened, "Your dad left because the devil got into him."

"The devil didn't get into him," I yelled, "You pushed him to it; you couldn't keep your man!"

I knew I shouldn't have said those words to her, but I was hurt. She grabbed my bag and threw it into the hallway. Nana started to scream, yelling at us to stop arguing. I picked up my bag and my box of sex toys. I threw my key on the floor as I walked out of the house. I didn't know where to go but I didn't want to stay in the house anymore. Tears clouded my eyes, I thought of staying in the town's hotel. But I changed my mind and turned into another street. I walked to Miss Willow's house and knocked on her door. Alice came to the door. She pulled me into her arms when she saw me. She let me into the house.

"What happened?" She asked.

"My mom kicked me out," I replied, "She saw my toys and she didn't want them under her roof."

Alice sighed as she walked me to the guestroom.

"Does she loathe sex toys?" Alice asked.

"My dad left her," I said, "I guess she's going through a lot, but she shouldn't have tried to take out her anger on me."

"Do you want anything?" Alice asked, "Coffee, tea or wine?"

"Wine," I replied.

I placed my stuff in the room and then I went into the kitchen with Alice. We drank wine as we sat there in the dark. All of a sudden, I started sobbing.

"Becky, honey, it's good to let it all out."

"I went on my first date today," I said, "It was so beautiful, why does she have to ruin this beautiful day for me?"

Alice grinned at me, "Today is a new day, it's already 12 am,"

I started laughing while tears ran down my cheeks, "Yeah, she ruined yesterday for me." "I am sorry darling," Alice said, "You can talk to her when she is calm. I guess she is heartbroken and also disappointed that her decent church-going daughter has a collection of sex toys. By the way, you do have some nice, exotic toys."

I grinned, "Oh Alice, what do I do? I said some mean words to her."

"Whenever you are angry, don't speak, or you may say things you wouldn't be able to take back." Alice said, "Whenever I am pissed, I lie down and bring myself to orgasm."

I giggled. "Oh, that's better."

"How was your date?" She asked.

I blinked my eyes as tears brimmed in them.

"It was beautiful," I replied, "Luke is so sweet."

Alice patted my hand, "Everything will be fine, and you just need to relax."

The wine made me feel relaxed and happy even though I knew it was alcohol induced happiness. It also made me incredibly horny. My body was tingling as sensations wrapped around my spine. The clapping sound of thunder suddenly filled the air; we listened to the rumbling sound as we sipped more wine. We finished the entire bottle of wine.

"I'm sorry for coming here unannounced," I said. "I didn't know where to go,"

She waved her hand, "I always appreciate any chance that I get to drink wine."

I laughed; I was handling my liquor well. I didn't know I could consume that much wine. Alice shut the kitchen window when the rain became windy. We said goodnight to each other, even though it was already morning. I went back into the guestroom and lay on the cool sheet. I became aroused as goosebumps appeared on my skin. I ran my fingers over my arms, brushing my fingers against the little bumpy flesh. I squeezed my breasts through my blouse, moaning. My hips shot upwards as I pressed a hand between my thighs. Sensations exploded in my head. I pulled off my blouse and my bra. The cold made my nipples stiff. I rubbed my fingers over my cold nipples until they felt warm.

I slid a hand into my skirt, pushing my panties to the side of my thighs. I brushed my fingers against my pussy lips. I bit my lips, moaning softly. I rubbed my clit as I continued to run a finger down my slit. I felt a cramping sensation in my abdomen when my finger slipped into my wet, warm pussy. My body started to quiver. I forgot about the fight with Mom, and I also forgot about Dad's betrayal. I took nipples clamps and pinned them to the tip of my nipples. A gigantic wave of pleasure washed over me. I bucked, writhing with pleasure. I started to slip my finger in and out of my horny pussy. My juice trailed down the inside of my thighs. I rubbed my clit, putting pressure on it with the heel of my palm. The nipples clamps made my nipples tingle.

I started to circle my finger on my clit, brushing the sides. Then I pinched my clitoral hood and I started to come. I pushed a butt plug into my anus, it started to vibrate against my tight rectum, sending hot waves of pleasure through me. I curved my finger inside me, rubbing the soft, slippery surface of my G-spot. My lips rounded, making a perfect O as my body started to shake. I yanked the nipple clamps off my nipples. Then, I squeezed my breasts, pinching my nipples with my fingers.

I started to come so hard, it felt so good, and I didn't want it to stop. I increased the vibrations of the butt plug; it stimulated every part of my anal walls. I took a vibrator and slipped it into my mouth. I licked the sides of the vibrator as I continued to give myself pleasure. I licked the frenum of the cock as if it was a real cock. I started bobbing my head as I suckled the cock, taking it all the way into my throat. I heard the rain hit the roof of the house. The cold in the room increased but I was warm and happy. I had wine in my belly, a finger in my pussy and a dildo in my mouth; what more could I ask for?

I flicked my finger against my clit; an amazing rush of adrenaline filled my body. My heartbeat increased as my heart started to pulsate. I drummed my fingers across my clit, it twitched a little. I started to buck my waist, crying so softly. When another wave of orgasm hit me all the muscles and nerves in my body relaxed.

I opened the window, the cold wind blasted into the room. I sighed as I started to play a song on my phone. I danced until I was sweating. Then I took a shower and went back to bed. I began to masturbate again. I caressed my body, brushing my fingers across every erogenous spot on my skin. I stroked the back of my neck, the sides of my breasts and ran a finger down my belly. I cupped my hand over my mound, it filled my palm. I moved my hand up and down, making my juice flow. I rubbed a finger around my anal rim; it opened up, sucking my finger into it. I heard a popping sound as my finger slide into my butthole. I thrust my finger in and out of my butthole, pushing it in until my knuckles brushed against my anal ring. I worked that finger into my butthole, pounding my ass so hard. I fondled my clit, crying out when sensations filled my body. I squeezed my pussy lips between my fingers, groaning.

The rain had stopped falling at this point, but the room was still cold. My clit was engorged. I started to finger my clit and my butthole at the same time. My orgasm rippled through me again. I rubbed my hand over my stomach, smiling from cheek to cheek. Then, I wrapped my arms around my body and drifted off to sleep.

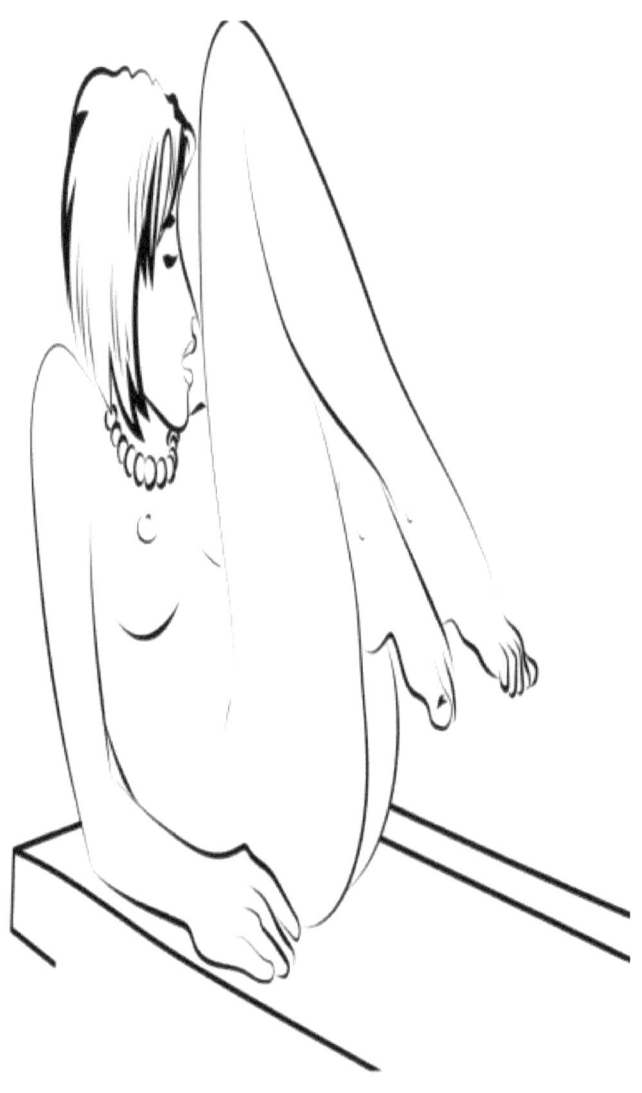

C

hapter XII

Sex Toys Don't Hurt Anyone

The ringtone of my phone woke me up; it was almost noon anyway. I had a terrible headache, and I was still drowsy. My skin was flushed. I just wanted to lie in bed all day. I reached for my phone; Mom's number reflected on the screen of the phone. I didn't want to talk to her or go back home yet. I thought she was trying to call me to say she was sorry. The call ended before I could make up my mind if I wanted to talk to her or not.

I called her back, holding my breath as it rang. Nana's voice came over the line. Her voice was trembling; she seemed agitated.

"Hello, Becky," She cried.

"Hello, nana," I said, "Why are you calling with Mom's phone?"

"Something terrible has happened," Nana said.

My heart skipped a beat as I jumped out of bed, "What happened?"

"Where are you?" Nana asked.

"Umm…I am staying with a friend." I replied, "What happened? Is Mom, okay?"

"I'm at the hospital, how soon can you get here?" Nana asked, "I don't think I can do this alone, please come."

"What happened? Why are you at the hospital?" I asked.

Questions raced through my mind. The call disconnected before I could ask Nana more questions. I pulled some clothes on and raced out of the room. Alice had made breakfast; the aroma was all over the apartment.

"Where are you going in such a rush?" She asked.

"My grandmother called," I replied, "She says something terrible has happened and she is at the hospital."

"Oh my god," Alice said, reaching for her car keys, "I'll drive you to the hospital, come on."

"How about your breakfast?" I asked.

"I don't mind skipping breakfast. Give me a minute to put everything into a microwave." She said. She rushed into the kitchen and came out.

Alice drove me to the hospital. I felt so guilty for whatever happened, even though I didn't know what it was. When the hospital came into view, Alice touched my arm.

"Everything will be alright," she said.

I nodded my head. "Do you want to come with me?"

"No, thanks," She replied with a smile, "I don't like hospitals."

"Thank you," I replied.

"You are welcome."

My legs trembled as I alighted from the car. I called Mom's number as I walked into the building. Nana told me she was in the intensive care unit. My heart started to pound in my ears as I walked down the hallway which led to the intensive care unit. My footsteps echoed in my ears. I was so scared that I couldn't breathe. My heart broke when I saw Nana standing outside a door, peering into the room through the glass window. I raced into her arms. I knew something had happened to Mom. I didn't know what it was, but I knew that something terrible had happened.

"What happened?" I asked. Then I peered through the glass, Mom was lying on the hospital bed. Some medical equipment was connected to her body. Her eyes were closed; she looked pale and frail.

"What happened to her?" I asked as tears trickled down my face.

"She tried to kill herself," Nana said.

My knees became weak, "Oh my god,"

"She's been holding in so much," Nana said, "She slashed her wrists."

My stomach churned. Nana started to sob, she had already lost a daughter, it would kill her if we lost Mom too.

"What if I didn't find her on time?" Nana asked, "She lost so much blood before I found her."

"What did the doctors say?" I asked. "Will she be alright?"

"She's in coma now," Nana sobbed.

"I am so sorry, Nana," I said, "I shouldn't have said those words to her."

"She needs us," Nana said, "We have to be there for her. She needs to know her family loves her."

"What do we do?" I asked.

"Get rid of those things she was upset about." Nana cried.

"What?" I cried, "Nana…they are just toys."

"Your mother needs you," Nana said, "You can't abandon her now. Just look at her, lying there so helpless. The doctors don't know when she will come around. What if something happens to her?"

"Nana, we have to be positive." I said, "Mom will be alright, she's going to be fine."

Nana took a deep breath, "When she comes around, I want you to ask for her forgiveness."

"Okay," I said, nodding my head.

"And you have to get rid of those toys now." She said.

"Sex toys don't hurt anyone," I said.

She turned her back to me, "Your mother needs you."

I turned around and walked out of the hospital.

When I got to Alice's, she didn't ask me anything; she only offered me a handkerchief and patted me on the back. I went into the guestroom and carried the box of sex toys. I didn't want to throw my precious toys away. I didn't want to go to bed at night, knowing that my toys were not with me. But my family needed me; it was a hard choice that I had to make. I loved my family, and I also loved my sex toys. I walked out of the house, cradling my precious box under my arm. I didn't want to throw them into the trashcan. I wished that I could give them to someone who would cherish them the way I did.

I didn't know which direction to go; I just kept walking until the river came into view. My heart ached as I left the box of sex toys on the river shore. Then I turned around and walked away without looking back.

ABOUT THE AUTHOR

Jiro Chatelain

Jiro's purpose in life is to ensure that there are laughter and happiness in every home and relationship. He has brought smiles to the faces of many people, and he has kept the love burning in several homes across the world. So, Jiro writes books, considering that you just read one of his books, so it makes perfect sense. He has been a ghostwriter for over four years, and he has touched so many lives through his books. Broken relationships have been rekindled through his counseling. He is dedicated to helping humankind and he is passionate about his family and friends. He is best known for writing non-fiction and erotica novel. In these four years as a ghostwriter, he has written on different genres, from romance books to subjects ranging from science fiction to personal finance. He is also an astute Entrepreneurs. Jiro Chatelain is also an investor, ranging from the stock market to Real Estate. He enjoys pie, as should all right-thinking people.

Jiro Chatelain

WWW.JIROCHATELAIN.COM

LUSTY VOYAGE I

www.ingramcontent.com/pod-product-compliance
Lightning Source LLC
Chambersburg PA
CBHW020051180626
46812CB00006B/2286